KOLCHAK™
The Night S...
the LOVECRAFTIAN
GAMBIT

MOONSTONE™

HACK

C.J. Henderson · Robert Hack

KOLCHAK:
The Night Stalker

the LOVECRAFTIAN GAMBIT

"What Every Coin Has"

story by
C.J. Henderson

illustrated by
Robert Hack

colored by
Jason Jensen

edited by **Joe Gentile**   design by **Erik Enervold**

creative consultant: **Mark Dawidziak**

Kolchak created by **Jeff Rice**

MOONSTONE

Joe Gentile – editor-in-chief
Dave Ulanski – art director
Lori G – editorial
Rory Bautista, Tim Ganz,
Max Cockrell & Mike Reynolds
–ground control–
Richard Dean Star
–special projects coordinator–
Tim Lasiuta
–research & development–
Joe Gentile & Dave Ulanski
–publishers–

visit us on the web at www.moonstonebooks.com

" The day of the printed word is far from ended.

Swift as is the delivery of the radio bulletin, graphic

as is television's eyewitness picture, the task of adding

meaning and clarity remains urgent.

People cannot and need not absorb

meaning at the speed of light."

Erwin Canham

" **S** o, at last, the great Carl Kolchak, striding forward into my kingdom." The speaker, one Marvin Richards, host of the wildly popular show *Challenge of the Unknown,* held his right hand out to the man being ushered into his office. "It's about time."

Richards was not in any way flattering to his colleague. They were both newsmen. They were also both newsmen who found themselves caught up with the strange, the bizarre, and even the supernatural on what seemed like a regular basis. The difference between these occurances was that while Kolchak stumbled across such events while looking for any kind of news to report, Richards was in the business of making the strange, the bizarre, and especially the supernatural, the news of the moment.

Richards' show was indeed wildly popular, but only in a fringe manner. Though the special telecasts he and his team had put together had nearly brought the world to actual disaster several times, they had survived the incidents professionally due to apathy. The truth be told, there were few who believed anything they saw on television anymore.

In a world where there existed educated people who did not believe man had ever landed on the moon, simply because their only proof of the event was television, it was reasonable to assume a show which took seriously everything from the Bermuda Triangle to UFOs was merely more fluff and nonsense–like programming about men who owned cars possessed by the spirits of their dead mothers, or ones about New York singles who could afford massive apartments in trendy Manhattan neighborhoods.

Carl Kolchak, a man with a preternatural sense about which side of the bread held the butter, advanced to the television personality's desk without hesitation. Taking the man's extended hand cleanly, he shook it neatly, something which caught Richards off-guard. Kolchak possessed a unique ability to read people, and could see that his host was the type to surround another's fingers with his hand rather than grasping their palm. Forcing the man to meet him squarely, Kolchak shook his hand easily, filling his face with a disarming grin.

"Oh, I agree, Mr. Richards. Someone should have made this happen years ago."

"Lora," the anchor called to the quite attractive assistant Kolchak had noticed on his way in, "get our guest here something to drink."

Richards confirmed that his guest was a Scotch drinker and gave Lora a signal that meant she should break out "the good stuff." The woman, comprised of soft curves and tense eyes, gave the anchorman a knowing nod and left the room silently. As she passed Kolchak, she let her tense eyes whirl, sending a message to the reporter that he was in shark-infested waters. It was the type of thing many kind and beautiful women did in his presence. She was back in a brief moment with two glasses which she handed to the pair as silently

as she did everything else. Working for *Challenge of the Unknown*, she had grown quite proficient at only being noticed when she wanted to be seen.

Richards and Kolchak made customary "thanks," sipped, made refreshed noises, and then settled into their chairs and commenced to duel. In truth they struck at each other with words only, and not three men in a hundred thousand would have noted anything more than polite conversation, but the pair were locked in combat nonetheless. Each pleasantry thrown forth, every compliment paid, all of it was merely window dressing for those in the cheap seats.

"I got to read that piece of yours last year on the last cruise of the S.S. Hanover—the werewolf story—great stuff. Loved that Penthouse idiot."

"You saw that? The full piece only ran in some crackpot giveaway rag. Nothing like what you boys do here."

Kolchak's manner was expansive, the motion of his hands open and gracious. The compliment implied was heart-felt, and that also caught Richards off-guard. The anchor nodded his head to show he knew how to take a compliment graciously. What he did not know how to

convey, or even if he should attempt such conveyance, was why the man across from him would be so honestly complimentary.

"So, tell me, good sir," Kolchak asked, his head tilted to the side, the reporter doing his best to project indifference in whatever answer would be forthcoming, "do you actually believe in werewolves?"

"I don't yet," answered Richards honestly. "But I'm willing to. Especially if you do."

"Oh really," answered Kolchak. The curve of his smile disarmingly friendly, he asked, "And why would that be?"

"Because my research team tells me that if Carl Kolchak says there's a monster in your pantry, you'd best believe him, or you'll be out of Oreos before you know it."

Richards then gave an exhaustive listing of things his guest had bumped against in the night, from the first vampire he had claimed to kill in Las Vegas through the alien he swore he knew had been captured in upstate New York. He talked of witches and zombies and things that shambled—some made of moss, some made of armor, and one comprised entirely of electricity.

Kolchak was impressed. Oh, he was aware of his host's credentials as well. Richards and his team had reported on everything from lethal leprechauns to the Jersey Devil, given the world new evidence of the creatures in Pascagoula, the Mad Gasser of Mattoon and the ever-elusive Spring Heel Jack—among others.

But then, it was easy to keep tabs on the reportings of the *Challenge of the Unknown* team. They were on television. Every week some fifty to eighty million people tuned in to watch as they showed footage of alien lights in the sky, opened lost crypts, or attempted to solve this or that supernatural riddle.

Kolchak took another sip of his Scotch, using the drink to buy himself a moment. He had yet to decide what Richards wanted, why he had been invited down from the seedy neighborhood of North Hollywood where his current paper, *The Hollywood Dispatch*, made its home, to the clean if somewhat boring Burbank neighborhood where *Challenge* was filmed. Holding his glass at an angle which allowed him to seem to study its contents while he actually studied his host's face, he said;

"Scotch this smooth, it's almost a crime to digest it."

"Thank you, Carl."

"It's also something guys like me don't get served unless someone has a reason. What's yours, Richards?"

The anchorman smiled.

"Right to the point—a Carl Kolchak trademark. I like that. But, more importantly, so will our viewers. That's why we brought you down here, Carl. We want you to be part of the *Challenge* team."

This time it was Kolchak who was caught off-guard. As good a poker-player as the anchorman across the desk from him, his well-disposed face revealed not a trace of his emotions, but surprised he was. As a reporter, his career had been in a downward spiral for some time. He might have started as a mere copy boy at the *Boston Globe*, but it was only a matter of a few years before he was one of the shining bright boys reaching toward the top of the NYC hot ink beat. He quickly brazened his way to such exalted heights by turning over large rocks and exposing massive piles of greed, sin and corruption. His only problem was he started believing his own press.

Forgetting that the torch of justice could only protect those who knew when it was time to breath in a little darkness, he had gone up against powers far too secure to be fazed by a lone crusader. In a patented manner polished since the time of Tammany Hall, New York had ushered him unceremoniously to the Lincoln Tunnel and shown him the way to Jersey. Grateful to have found himself in the Garden State merely rumpled, but unbroken, he headed westward, managing to find a paper in Chicago that would take him in. Setting fires under the local Democratic bosses his first week bought him exit from the Windy City with alarming speed.

It took several more righteous disasters to land him in Las Vegas, and that was where his descent had become complete.

"What do you say, Carl?"

What could he say? In Vegas Kolchak he had been run out of town once more, and once more it had been by politicians, but their fear of what he had discovered had been different. He had stumbled onto a truth about terrors in the night that modern, godless men were unequipped to handle. He had torn the curtain of scientific sanctimony aside, and the man behind it to whom no one had wished to pay attention had turned out to be a monster of unbelievable proportions. After that, a number of lesser positions had followed, all terminating the reporter after he found his way to some other nightmare the world at large wished left undisturbed.

"Why me, Marv? I mean, obviously I have some guesses, but I'd like to hear what you have to say."

"Why you?" asked Richards in immediate response. "Dude–who else? You're Carl Kolchak. You're an Internet legend. Take a look at the kind of shows we do here. You're right up our alley. We couldn't invent a reporter more perfect."

Kolchak moved his back further into the deceptive comfort of his chair, ignoring its enticing allure, working hard to keep his wits about him in the face of Richards' expertly-ladled praise. The reporter had spent a lot of time having his teeth kicked in by his chosen profession. Accolades, especially those of the runaway variety, were something that always made him suspicious. Eventually, however, the two were able to cut through the preliminaries and get down to the inevitable negotiations.

Richards laid his cards on the table. The world only had so much bizarre news. At least, only so much they could find every week. They had come up with rehashes and conspiracy theories and homages that had delighted their core demographic, but they were running dangerously close to repeating themselves one too many times. They needed something fresh. They needed something new. They needed Carl Kolchak.

It had been decided that the best way to ease the reporter into the television way of doing things would be to let him host his own retrospective segment.

The camera would move in slowly on him as he sat in some kind of mock 1940s newsroom set, and Carl would begin to narrate this or that of his adventures. Actors would portray him and the things he met in re-enactment segments. Add in a bit of location shooting, a few computer-facilitated special effects, and suddenly a full quarter of every week's broadcast was going to be not only a ratings bonanza, but cost effective beyond their producers' wildest dreams.

Indeed, the savings alone over the costs of trying to find new, hard supernatural or preternatural news was so extraordinary that the salary which they could afford to offer Kolchak was outlandish enough to allow him to quip;

"Is this per show or per season?"

Richards laughed easily, Kolchak joined in, and the Night Stalker segment of *Challenge of the Unknown* was born. The two men argued over the title for a short while, but the anchor explained that, A, it was a "cool" label because Carl stalked the night for the truth, and, B, the producers and the head of the network were in love with the sound of it. Still smiling, Kolchak drained the last dregs of his third tumbler of scotch and decided for the money they were offering, he would be the Night Stripper if they wanted.

While he stretched out in his chair, waiting for Richard's lovely Lora to fetch him another scotch, the back of his mind reminded him that he was not the first human being to make such an offer in jest, only to be called on it later.

The first two days of shooting went as smoothly as possible. Richards did a stretch that would both intrigue the audience and kill time. Kolchak then repeated what the anchor had said in his own words–his own words carefully edited, scanned by legal, scanned by standards and practices, scanned by the sponsors–and then narrated the tale. That Richards had chosen to shoot their passages on a two person set–less time-efficient, more costly–told the reporter that at long last there just might be some value to others being associated with him. It was a thought he had not been able to entertain for a number of years.

If forced to answer, Kolchak would have to admit that the show's small amount of status made him feel ... good—no ... expansive. For the first time, in a long time, Carl Kolchak was firing on all cylinders. Oh, he had never lost his nose for news—his instincts for following a story to its end had never failed him. What had left him, however, was the joy of it all.

Finding it again was making him practically giddy.

"Marv, my boy, my friend, mine amigo," he called out, big arms animated at his sides, "I think that last one went great. What did you think? When I paused at the end, trying to get

across what I actually felt, how I froze for that second when that damn medicine man loomed over me—did you feel it?"

"I did," answered Richards honestly.

And once more, the anchor marveled at his honesty. He had been chilled by Kolchak, spell-bound. Actually frightened. He did wonder, however, if what he felt would translate to the home audience. His new team member was proving to be a natural story-teller, but, he asked himself, was it enough by itself merely to hear the reporter's words, or was his presence necessary.

The notion made him ponder over how they would eventually cover their bets—acres of fast-cut, weird angle graphics, or lots of tight shots of Kolchak himself, stark background, intense close-ups of his eyes and moving lips. He stared at the reporter for a long moment, then said;

"You know, Carl, you've got a really honest face. It's like something, I don't know, like it belongs on Rushmore. I think you're going to make people stop and think. Not because you have facts and irrefutable evidence. But, because you're believable, I think you may actually come across as... genuine."

"And that's good—right?"

"It would be just you and Oprah."

Kolchak grinned. As he basked, Richards gave him a further splash of sunlight.

"All that money we're paying you...?"

"What about it?"

"You were robbed."

The reporter laughed. It felt good—twenty-years earlier good, copy boy good. He was finally in the big time—the big enough time. And it was coming fast.

Incredibly fast. Just four days earlier he had been to Richards' office for the first time. They had had scripts ready for him to look at before he even knew they wanted to meet with him. Scripts, he knew, they could easily film without him. The segments would not have resonated as fully as they were shaping up to with him actually there, but they could have used his career without him—legally and a lot less cheaply—if they had had to do so.

Thus Carl Kolchak gratefully accepted the fun and fringes that came with playing ball.

He had walked out of his first meeting with Richards with the equivalent of six months pay from the *Dispatch* for which the wonderful world of television only expected two days work. He knew he was selling off his life on the block, but he was happy to do it. They wanted ten days total out of him, and that was just to get their test segments ready. If they went over with the audience the way everyone expected them to, then he would be back in the studio for two days a week for a minimum of ten months.

Carl Kolchak had finally found a ball game where he could excel. He was ready to play round after round with Richards' and his crew, a swell bunch of kids he had grown quite fond of actually–especially the tantalizing, blue-eyed Lora–for as long as the park was opened. He was happy and content, and, he suddenly realized, he still had upcoming the pleasure of telling one Tony Vincenzo that he could fetch his own corned beef sandwiches in the future.

Carl, my lucky, lucky boy, he whispered within his head, for once you've got it made. What could possibly go wrong now?

"Hey, superstar," called out Richards, "Come see this."

Kolchak crossed the studio to where Marvin Richards was studying something hidden from the reporter's view. A cardboard shipping box had been positioned in the center of a research table, it's top flaps pulled back to reveal its contents. Mounds of packing peanuts scattered all around gave the impression that something extremely fragile waiting inside the box.

"What is it?"

"Something one of our research teams sent over from..." Richards searched for a mailing label, then shrugged, answering, "I can't find the paperwork now, but it's from somewhere in the Middle East."

"Well, that at least tells me where it's from, sorta," answered Kolchak, using his let's-get-it-together tone, "but not what it is."

"What it is..." said Richards, pulling a rectangular shape from the box, Styrofoam peanuts spilled in every direction as he did so, "... is a book."

Kolchak, Lora and several others waited with varying degrees of anticipation as the anchor carefully cut his way through some fourteen layers of bubble wrap surrounding the object which did finally reveal itself to be a book——but a book like none any of them had ever seen

before. It was a large, dark thing, long and thick and smelling of antiquity. It had rusting metal clasps holding its too-soft covers together, two thin, wire bound slats of spongy mahogany covered in more than a dozen layers of hole-worn leather of a type none present could identify.

"Smells like it might be fairly old," said Kolchak. "Are you sure its safe to open it here? Without the proper climate controls, I mean?"

"Smells too much like ratings to me not to open it," answered Richards, his eyes twinkling. Then, realizing the reporter might have something, he immediately called a cameraman over to begin a documentary-style filming of the opening. He also went so far as to put the book back in the box and to cover it once more with packing peanuts. Then, camera in place, the anchor pulled the book forth, cut the carefully retaped bubblewrap, and then urged a sincere first viewing reaction out of all those seeing the book for the second time.

"Here it is, the granddaddy of all magical books."

As Richards carefully opened the bound volume to its first page, Kolchak read the largest words centered there, assuming they were its title.

The *Kitah al-Azif.*"

"Just one of its names, Carl." Richards handed the reporter a list his overseas contact had sent along with the book. Kolchak scanned it, looking for a name he recognized. He saw more than one.

"*El Libro de lis Normos*, Book of the Essence of the Soul, *Cultus Maleficarum, Liber Logaeth, Necronomicon Ex Mortis*——*Necronomicon*? This thing is supposed to be the Necronomicon?"

"*Necronomicon, Necremicon, Necromicon, Necronemicon*, a lot of names, but all the same book."

Kolchak let out a low whistle. He had heard of the book more than once——met men who would have murdered countless innocents to get their hands on it. While investigating other cases with a supernatural bent, he had heard rumors about the volume's contents which had truly frightened him. Not that he had not been frightened by much he had seen since Las Vegas, but the occasional witch or zombie, they had frightened him personally, made him fear for his immediate safety. What he had heard about the book on the table before him had made him fear for the world.

"All the same book all right," agreed Kolchak, "and a Hell of a book——pun intended. Just what were you thinking of doing with this thing?"

"What you do with anything that's news," answered the anchor, his eyes firmly glued to the mottled yellow page before him. "Put it on the air. Discovery of the world's oldest, most awesome book of magic. King of the sorcerous texts, learn how to bewitch the girl next door, chant your way to riches——I'm telling you, we'll knock that goddamned History Channel into the basement."

Richards began to thumb through the book, carefully turning one clump of ancient pages after another. None present could read the book, of course. Not only was it in Arabic, but the dialect was, according to the page of information Kolchak continued to scan, some three thousand years old. Still, Richards' excitement continued to mount at an even rate with Kolchak's apprehension. As the reporter noted that the book was reputed to have multiple sections on summoning things from beyond, the anchor exclaimed;

"Wow——look at this little beastie."

Richards let the page fall open so that all present could see the illustration. Lora gasped, turned away, started to turn back, and then crossed the room to sit down removing herself from the immediate area. The cameraman, a hefty fellow famous for having eaten a sandwich while filming an apartment fire which consumed fifteen people, blinked hard, shuddered, and then leaned inward and sideways to get a better look. The screams of people having their flesh burned from their bodies had not caused him to blink, but the crudely rendered, thirty centuries old drawing before him made him not only blink, but it caused him to forget his camera.

None at the table would have blamed him.

"What the..."

"And that's not the only one."

With the caution of an archeologist brushing away the dust of ages, Richards turned the pages one by one in that section, showing off an increasingly bizarre menagerie of things that seemed beyond the realm of the human imagination. One of the line producers, a man who had paid some attention during his bible studies as a youth in Nebraska before he escaped to

college and the big city beyond, commented;

"I don't get it. I thought all these old types described demons as having the head of a turtle and the legs of a bird and the claws of a lobster——ten dog heads on a lion's body with the wings of an eagle, stuff like that. This guy makes Hieronymus Bosch look like Peter Max."

The creatures were all nightmares, horrors sketched in blackness, things all tentacles and fangs, armored legs that ended in tearing points, heads filled with razored mouths and piercing eyes, horrid things, damned things...

"Evil."

"Let's not go all Stevie King here now, Carl."

"What?" The reporter cocked his head to one side, throwing his gaze at Richards like a battering ram. "Am I getting too judgmental for you? What the hell else would you call those things? Are you actually looking at those things? That's no collection of Macy Thanksgiving Day balloons; I can guarantee you that!"

Richards turned another page. What appeared there looked more like an ink stain than anything else. It had folds to it, looming strands of essence which appeared something like appendages, but it was of such loose design it made a jellyfish look like Dorothy's Tin

Woodman. As the crowd stared, an intern called to Richards.

"Sir, there's a Mr. Penes here to see you."

"Now that is what I call timing," responded the anchor. His well-known confidence swelling past its normal levels, Richards motioned for the man to be brought over immediately. Ushered into the already growing crowd was a slightly smaller than average individual with a slender frame and light green eyes.

"Dr. Randel Peles, yes?" When the newcomer agreed to the label, Richards announced that he had called in the good doctor, a para-psychologist of no small renown, to consult with them on the very subject at hand.

"I expected the book today, but I didn't expect you until tomorrow, doctor."

"You had mentioned that the book would arrive today, and I saw no reason to waste time." The man's voice held an excitement that was positively gleeful. Trying to use his slight frame as a wedge, he motioned with his shoulder to the crowd as he asked, "Is that it? May I see it?"

The crowd parted and the smaller man came forward. He stared at the open page intently, his hands busy in his pockets. As Richards went to turn a page Penes reached out and slapped his hand, chiding him for not using the type of plastic gloves he himself was

pulling from his jacket. As he pulled them on, the anchor said;

"Oh, sure. Oil from the skin, hurts old paper——right?"

"Yes."

Penes drawled the word with the tone of one agreeing with a child's nonsense simply to silence them. Taking his own chance with the man, Kolchak asked;

"Can you tell us what this thing is we're looking at, sir?"

"Nyogtha——a minor deity reported to inhabit underground caverns. Few followers these days, black witches, that ilk."

"So…" Kolchak struggled to word his next question, "that's supposed to be a living… being?"

"A being?" Penes rolled the concept over in his head for a moment. Still staring at the page, he answered, "Living darkness would be more like it. It's an embodiment of shadow, a blob of black hunger that throws out pseudopods to entrap those who get too near. Sucks out their souls, supposedly its victims' life energies fuel it. Just another vampire, really. The text below is the binding spell to summon it."

The room temperature chilled appreciably despite the studio's excellent climate controls. As the small man busied himself with the ancient text on the table, those around him found themselves in varying states of shock and wonder.

"The text below is the binding spell to summon it."

Penes had said the words so casually, so matter-of-factly, as if reading off the next paragraph of instructions for hooking up a set of speakers, or the next line of directions on a road trip to Toledo. No one tried to kid themselves about his tone.

There was no doubt in any of their minds that, no matter what the truth, Dr. Randel Penes believed that he could bind and summon the black amorphous horror on the page before them.

"Really?"

"That's what it says." Penes answered Richards' question with an innocent tone, as if he did not care one way or the other. Catching the truth in both men's voices, Kolchak thrust his way into the conversation.

"Now wait a minute here. Just what are you two talking about? You, you're not going to

try and, and bring that thing here are you?"

"Carl," answered Richards' smoothly. "That's what we do. We bring people the news about the world beyond. If there really is one, and we can prove it, we're just doing our job."

"Well then," countered the reporter, "how about a special on electronic voice phenomena, or that last rain of frogs in Omaha?"

"Because this is bigger," answered the anchor simply. "This is sweeps week stuff. This is beat-the-networks stuff. This is the kind of thing they give you an Emmy for."

"Or a headstone."

Richards took Kolchak by the shoulder and gently steered him away from the table. His staff stayed where they were, recognizing the anchor's style. The reporter needed soothing, and their boss would work his usual magic. For the most part, they were content to simply wait for someone to tell them what to do while the ticking clock continued to swell their bank accounts.

"Carl," the anchor started, his voice smooth and low, friendly and concerned, "I think I know what you're worried about..."

"If you were thinking I was worried about us all getting ripped to shreds by some

damned three thousand year old nightmare then you might actually be on to something."

"Carl, now work with me here for a moment. We both believe in the unknown. We've seen it; we've touched it, been chased down alleys by it, the whole nine yards——yes?"

Kolchak nodded, willing to give Richards that much.

"All right. We've seen these things happen over and over, and yes–people have suffered, and people have died. Agreed?"

"I'm not sure how this is building your case, Marvin, but you've got me there. Yes——yes, indeed——every single goddamned time I've come up against things like this, yes, people have died.

But the reason I haven't is because I always come in *after* they died. Because they've died. I get the advantage that way—see? I already know something is going on." Richards put his hand up as an interrupting gesture, but Kolchak brushed it aside, growling;

"But now, you—you want to give that advantage to someone else. You want us to be the ones who start something. Well, you brought me in here for my experience, and so I'm telling you right now—in my experience the ones who start this crap are the ones who do the dying!"

"Yes, right again," Richards agreed. "But look at why they start it. They're looking for power, or everlasting life, or a romance they have no right to. These things are always started by people after something they don't deserve."

Kolchak pursed his lips. He did not want to, but he had to admit that so far the anchor was making sense.

"All I'm saying Carl is that we're newsmen. We don't have these types of greed. Sure we want to be rich; we want beautiful women in our beds——we're human. But we're not willing to trade in blood to get them. We're talking the people's right to know here. It's our sacred duty to report the facts. But, we can't just show the book and tell people that it can summon creatures. They need proof."

Again Kolchak considered what was being said. Richards might be treading dangerous, but that was the name of their game. He had covered wars, been on the scene at police shoot outs, been threatened by gangsters, union reps and politicians—not that he saw much difference in any of the three—danger was part of any real reporter's life.

"People have lost their faith in everything, Carl. God doesn't work miracles anymore. People are just as likely to believe in the healing powers of crystals as they are prayer to any of the accepted, government-approved saviors. If we bring something like this on stage, make it do a few tricks, suddenly we've torn the curtain aside. We've given people hope, proved there's an afterlife. For Christ's sake, Carl, we'll be bigger than the Pope, with an option for a two-season pick-up."

Kolchak was just beginning to think Richards might really be onto something when the first screams tore through the studio.

Both men's heads jerked, first in the direction of Lora who had let out the initial, piercing shriek, and then around again toward what she had seen which had elicited her terror. Richards jerked his head several times, his hands shaking, lips forming soundless words. Kolchak's hands automatically searched his chest for his camera. His mind knew it had to be there somewhere, but it could not redirect his eyes to join the hunt. They were too busy staring, absorbing, trying to comprehend. At the same moment the back of his mind

shouted that the camera was with his other clothes, that he was still wearing those things given him by the wardrobe department, his conscious mind put together what must have happened.

"Son of a bitch—that little bastard went and summoned that Nyogtha thing!"

Other senses began to feed him information. An insidious odor began to fill the room, a scent filled with equal parts of rotting honey and boiling tar-vaguely musky, reptilian and nauseating. His ears picked up the sounds of more than one person heaving, the liquified remains of their catered lunches splashing against the studio floor. His own throat lurched, giving him a taste of bile, but he bit back the sensation, then threw his arms down rigid at his sides. Making fists, he steeled his body, pulling his nerves back under his own command. Driving the fear from his mind, he forced himself to see clearly, to ignore the growing gelatinous mass of iridescent blackness, and to search for the real cause of their problems.

At the table across the room, he spotted Randel Penes, his hands on the ancient text.

A violet, pulsing glow was ascending from the book upward along his arms, even as a faint pink one spiralled downward from his shoulders, flowing into the pages. Knowing he had to separate the para-psychologist from the text as quickly as possible, the reporter raced across the room and threw himself into the smaller man.

Penes went down in a tumble as the darkness in the center of the room spasmed, throwing forth great roping tentacles of something neither liquid or solid. Three of them caught hold of Richards' hefty cameraman, dragging him across the room as if he had no more substance than a bag of tissues.

Pink life fled the man's body in rivers, torn from his body so harshly he had not the time to scream before Nyogtha had sucked his dry of memories, ambitions, hopes, joy, and all the other human tastes it loved so dearly.

"Get off me, you great oaf."

Penes snarled, shoving at Kolchak with a strength the reporter found amazing. As the smaller man hurried to his feet, Kolchak followed him, shouting;

"Sorry, but I had to break the connection between you and the book. It was, I could see it, it was grabbing onto you, stealing from you, filling——"

"You clod," Penes interrupted, wheeling abruptly to slap Kolchak away from him. "Of course it was filling me; of course I was being drawn into it. What do you think I came here for? To be on television?"

The cameraman's body crashed to the floor at that moment, a dry and withered collection of desiccated bones and skin. The sound of its contact was only that of a small collection of wooden clothes pins dropped from a modest height, but it was enough to snap the others out of their shock. Everyone else who had been around the table threw themselves away from the book, Penes, the area in general, with reckless abandon. Several crashed into each other. Others tripped over cables, or equipment, or those who had crashed into one another. More than half of the crowd found themselves sprawled on the floor, crying and screaming and beating against one another as the pseudopods came searching for more victims.

"You mean," shouted Kolchak, "you did this on purpose?"

"Nyogtha is a perfect servitor for such a moment. Not too big. Easily satisfied, easily dispelled. A most excellent tool to allow me to steal the *Kitah al-Azif* from you fools."

Carl Kolchak was not an overly brave man. But, he was a practical one, and he knew that the thing eating its way through the crowd in the center of the room would get to him sooner or later if he did not do something to stop it. And, since he could not do anything to stop such a monster directly, he did the only other thing he could. Pulling back his left arm, he thanked his Polish heritage for a strong back and snapping good punch and let loose for the doctor's head.

His arm slammed into a wall of electrical torment which sent him flying away from Penes, knocking him to his knees, blind with pain.

"Really, you should never have let me touch the book again."

Kolchak tried to stand, fell sideways, recoiling in agony as his over-heated body came in contact with the tile floor below.

"You did catch me off-guard once, but did you think me so foolish as to be unprepared for you by now?"

Head ringing, mouth tasting of salt, the reporter clawed his way to his feet, forcing his eyes to open one at a time. Behind him, he heard people screaming, could feel their lives being yanked from their bodies, could smell their ashen remains floating in the air.

"I've waited decades for some rich bastards like you to bring this prize to me. Sanctimonious hypocrite–the only way you got your hands on this was to pay off one terrorist sect or the other. Funding murderers so you can sell cars and toilet paper. Your sick world is going to end now. Once I've had time to really study what you fools have delivered unto me, once I've brought forth those great old ones who truly have the power to cleanse all the Earth, then..."

Kolchak shut his mind to Penes' words. There was nothing to learn there. Following that, he harshly closed himself to the slaughter behind him. He could do nothing to help those being absorbed, stolen, violated on every conceivable manner possible. Not if he could not think.

Think, Carl, his mind shouted at him, pull yourself together. You've stopped worse than this. What are you missing? Think you stupid Mick bastard——*think*!

There were no weapons in the building. Thanks to California's gun paranoia, even the

security force was unarmed. He could not touch Penes. Any contact with the man would simply send him flying once more.

But I've got to stop him, Kolchak thought. He's the one in control of the monster. He's got the power. He's...

And then, the reporter's mind clicked and he took note of the one fact both he and Penes had missed up until then. Without hesitation, Kolchak lashed out and kicked the table before him into the doctor. A flurry of packing peanuts filled the air as Penes stumbled backwards, his hands leaving the ancient book.

Instantly the reporter threw himself upward and staggered forward. Penes caught himself, threw himself back toward the table, but he was too late. Kolchak forced himself in between the doctor and the table, grabbed up the volume and then flung it across the room, deep into the shadowy folds of Nyogtha.

"You, you, you... what have you done?"

Rather than answer the raging Penes, Kolchak stepped forward and grabbed the man by his coat, certain that without contact with his text that his spell of protection would be

broken. Spinning the smaller man around, Kolchak hustled him forward, shouting;

"You want your goddamned book so bad——*go get it!*"

And then, the reporter shoved Penes as hard as he could, flinging him into the waiting tendrils of writhing blackness which sucked on his screams as happily as it had everyone else's. Unlike all the others, however, the doctor's essence seemed to hold some special flavor for the nightmare. As quickly as the shimmering darkness had appeared, it splintered and folded inward on itself, then disappeared, leaving behind several small smudges on the floor no scientific agency would be able to identify, an indelible aroma which would not completely leave the center of the studio completely for some seventeen weeks, and the casually abandoned remains of some eighteen human beings and one now quite liquified book of dark wisdom.

"So, no changing your mind, Carl?"

Kolchak sat across from Marvin Richards in the anchor's office, a last tumbler of expensive Scotch in his hand. As the reporter had hoped as strongly as he had suspected,

capturing the human so presumptuous as to summon it had been enough to satisfy Nyogtha. Like a bear disturbed in its den by a pack of foolhardy campers, once the one clumsy enough to step on its paw was dispatched it was glad enough to retreat to its beloved caverns. No one else present claimed to know what had happened to Penes.

"No hope at all?"

An explanation had been offered that the thing had simply grabbed the doctor on its own, then disappeared. The police, tired of the headaches caused them by that particular Burbank studio, were happy to confuse the book purchasd from terrorists and the doctor as folks working hand in hand. Penes was charged as a mass murderer and the case was officially closed.

"No," Kolchak answered, wondering if the anchor could possibly be kidding, "I don't think so. I should have known television isn't really my medium."

Richards sighed. Spreading his hands wide across his desk, he confided, "you know those scripts will get made as news items. What you've claimed will be reported, an actor will play you; we'll get what we want—most of what we want—and you..."

The anchor made a gesture laden with futility. Kolchak nodded, then took another satisfying sip from his glass.

"You could use the money, couldn't you?"

"A man can always use money, Marvin," agreed the reporter. "But when it becomes more important to him than self-respect, then as my father used to say, 'he might be needing a kick in the pants more.'"

"Could be, could be," Richards agreed with a small laugh. "Me, I lost my need for self-respect along about the time I nailed my third super-model."

"Well, what do you need with self-respect," asked Kolchak, his tone intended to imply he was more teasing than serious, "after all, you're in television."

Richards howled, banging his fist against his desk. Suddenly all the wrangling with the police, the coroner's office and the network's legal department seemed as if it were nothing. He even forgot the sensation of unconsciously urinating on himself when his mind told him he was about to die. All of it faded from memory as what would have been an insult to anyone else made him feel refreshed and whole.

"Don't feel all that high and mighty, Carl. Wasn't it Mark Twain who said something about becoming a newspaperman because he couldn't find honest work?"

Kolchak grinned, took another wondrous sip of the oh, so tempting Scotch, then answered, "Indeed it was. But, it was also Twain who said 'Get the facts first, then you can distort 'em as you please." As Richards stared forward, the reporter explained;

"Things happen too quickly in your world for me, Marv. This show you have here, this isn't the news, it's a dispensary for sensation. I won't argue that that's what most newspapers have become, I'll just say I have to be somewhere where I at least have the option to study a story, to try and get the facts before I rush headlong into something."

Kolchak took his next to last sip, saving just enough of the liquid gold for a final swallow, then said;

"There's two sides to every coin and journalists are supposed to find them both. People died here because you didn't take the time to check out this Penes. Or the book. You believe in this stuff and you know what we're dealing with here. I understand what kind of pressures you're under, and I'm not saying I couldn't be dragged under by them, too. I'm human, and I haven't nailed my first super-model yet. But then, I don't nail women, Marv..." Kolchak let the phrase hang just the right amount of seconds, then finished;

"I make love to them."

Richards shook his head, smiling in defeat as Carl Kolchak finished his drink. The reporter had just saved the anchor's life and Richard's was not about to argue with him. He was also about to walk away from more money than he could have contemplated a week earlier because of his principles. The anchor could not pretend to understand, but he knew enough to be impressed. As Kolchak rose to leave, he shook hands with Richards, noting that the anchor extended his hand cleanly, giving him a smooth handshake.

Then, as they broke contact, Richards held up the bottle from which they had been drinking and offered, "Carl, parting gift, take the rest of the Scotch."

"No need, Marv." When the anchor looked slightly hurt, the reporter admitted;

"I've already got a full bottle in my camera bag." With a sweeping gesture, Richards bowed humbly to the master. Then, he sat back in his chair which he loved so dearly because it was more expensive than the one the head of the network had in his office, and began to rummage through his files.

If only, he thought, I can find the number of that reporter who claims to be chasing that big green monster...

While, at the same time, Carl Kolchak stopped at the lovely Lora's desk, asking both if she were ready for their date, and also if she minded if they picked up an extra lean corn beef sandwich for a dear friend.

"Your friend can't pick up his own sandwiches?"

"I'm going to have you deliver it. It'll just make him wonder what I've been up to."

"And," asked Lora, the tension in her blue eyes remarkably calmed as she looked at the reporter, "just what are you going to be up to?"

"Why, ma'am," answered Kolchak, taking her arm gallantly, "that, of course, will be up to you." •

KOLCHAK:
The Night Stalker

the LOVECRAFTIAN HORROR

story by
C.J. Henderson

illustrated by
Jaime Calderon

edited by Lori G

design & prepress by Erik Enervold/Simian Brothers Creative

creative consultant: Mark Dawidziak

Kolchak created by Jeff Rice

MOONSTONE

Joe Gentile - editor-in-chief
Dave Ulanski - art director
Lori G & Garrett Anderson
-editorial-
Greg Gass & Mike Renolds
-ground control-
Kathleen O'Brien - web master
Joe Gentile & Dave Ulanski
-publishers-

visit us on the web at www.moonstonebooks.com

A camera went off in my eyes.
"Quite a story, Carl."
It was not the worse thing that had happened to me that morning, and I was fairly certain it would not be the last. In fact, the growing sarcasm being thrown at me by the back of my mind was letting me know that being blinded was probably going to be the high point of my day.

"Buckin' for that Pulitzer again, eh, Mr. Kolchak?"
I smiled as graciously as I could. And, I must admit, for a complete and total fraud I pulled it off admirably. Still, the knowledge that I could so shame-facedly make complete and utter fools out of those closest to me with a pack of bald-faced lies was not making me feel any better over having done it. Perhaps I should explain.

What I had wanted for more years than I care to remember had finally happened. I, Carl Kolchak, had finally broken a titanic story. I was suddenly a household word, a journalistic hero. And, the only part of that which bothered me, the truth so diligently being ignored by all those gathered was that I was being honored for a story I really didn't write. Oh, much of what appeared under my by-line is true... -sort of. The way the story of the Immaculate Conception is true.

Sort of.

As everyone in the staff room continued to cheer and pass around the level of champagne the offices of the Hollywood Dispatch can afford, I accepted my fraudulent role as one of the world's best and bravest news hounds.

It was a bribe I had been handed by a grateful government, and which I had accepted because it was the only thing anyone in my situation could have done. It made me feel lousy, and after another round of humiliating hugs and embarrassing handshakes, I finally managed to corral my editor and force him into his office.

Now, for those who have not had the pleasure of his company, Tony Vincenzo is a round sort of man, a small, dried-out Brooklyn-born Sicilian. That he now lived in California only goes to show how hard the proud people of Brooklyn will work to disassociate themselves from those with whom they do not wish to tolerate any longer. Happy with me for once, he turned into a less honest version of the self I had learned to tolerate over the years. Luckily, life had handed me a way of cooling his ardor for my talents.

Getting him behind his desk, I told him to sit down. Drink in hand, he slid behind the great wooden bear of a desk he has dragged with him from one office to the next and looked at me as if

he was already well beneath happy with me. Caring less about such things than ever, I pulled a piece of paper from my pocket as I told him;

"Vincenzo, you may have all the fame and glory you want for the Dispatch that you ever dreamed was possible, and this may be a thing of great joy for you–"

"Just tell me why you dragged me in here, Kolchak."

"I'm getting to that part. I know you're a very happy man right now, quite pleased with us scooping the world, but I have to tell you how it happened. Where it all came from."

"Carl, please ..."

"No," I told him, working up a note of sincerity I didn't know I could reach, "you have to let me do this. Someone has to know the truth."

"Oh, God." That was his immediate reaction. He stared at me for a very intense second, his beetle-like eyes squinting harshly, then he raised his glass as if he were going to toss the whole thing down in a gulp. Something stayed his hand, though, and he started to speak again as if just changing his tone could send me off in a different direction.

"Now, Carl," he started, "you're not going to spoil my good mood, are you? I mean, please reconsider any such actions." The happiness was fizzing out of him, like air escaping from a birthday balloon.

Taking a long sip from his tumbler, he added;

"I deserve a good mood, you know. I mean, let's face it, ever since I met you I've had so few of them. You don't want to pull this all away from me, now–do you?"

I knew it wasn't fair, what I was about to do to him. But, it was more unfair for me to live a lie, and I knew he would feel the same when I was done. Of course, the back of my mind reminded me, I'd been sure I knew a lot of other things a few days earlier, as well. Forcing myself to refrain from any further caustic comments, I simply told him;

"I'm going to read you something, Vincenzo. It's a statement I left with the Department of the Navy."

The little, clown doll eyes of my editor rolled in their plastic ball sockets. As he stared at me, I cleared my throat, then asked that he let me finish before he interrupted. As he threw back the last of his drink, I began reading.

"'On Saturday, August 17th of this year, the United States Navy did swiftly and with courage to spare, launch an invasion on the coastal region to the north of Rogers, California. Despite the resultant loss of American lives and the significant property damage that ensued, in this reporter's

opinion, they had no other choice. The marines that landed on what can only be described as Hell's beachhead that night fought their way through an invasion force the equal to any that has ever been assembled at any time throughout history.

"'I say this under no coercion; this I swear on Menchen's grave. No warrior group has ever faced a more terrible enemy than these men. None has ever gone into combat for a higher principle. What little I was witness to was brutal, twisted-maddening. And I mean truly maddening. It has been rumored lately that those who died in that hideous combat were the lucky ones.

"'I can not comment on such sentiments as that. I still feel comfortable enough to keep thinking the average man's idea of sanity is obtainable; but then, it wasn't so bad for me. I didn't see what those men saw. It must be understood, however, though I walked the battlefield, I was no combatant. I came in after the real fighting. And that, in all honesty, was unnerving enough. The things I saw on the front our boys took, that Boschian nightmare that used to be just another little, useless American town, that was bad enough. I pity anyone who has to carry any more than what little I saw in their heads.

"'These men and women, they saved more than jobs or property or even lives. They did more than

keep the upcoming weekend carefree for the rest of us; it must be understood that these men saved, at the absolute least, our entire planet, and they sacrificed their lives and their minds to do it. They are, in my opinion, the greatest heroes of modern times.

"'And, unless George really slew a dragon, unless Arthur really did tangle with demons and gods, unless you're saying that Homer wasn't a teller of tales but a chronicler of actual events, then the sailors that bombarded the American coastline, the Marines who went into those horrible caverns, are most likely the bravest men who ever lived. If I were putting these words down on the official record for my paper, if I were allowed to print the pictures I have, the things that I know, I'd be the most famous reporter in the world.

"'But, I don't, and I won't. For, I am stating here in this record that I believe that in this particular instance, the government is right. There are some secrets that need to be kept. I can scarcely believe I'd ever agree to something like this. To me, the public has a sacred right to know what's happening around them. What things are affecting their lives. I've never seen a cover-up I could agree to ... until now.

"'Thus, I am stating for the record that I, Carl Kolchak, agree that the United States Navy attack at Kresse was a right and proper action. And that the wild rumors about monsters and "the creature

from the black lagoon," "batmen," and all the rest, are total bunk. If my reputation for trying to get people to believe in the outlandish and the supernatural, et cetera, means anything, then let me state once again that the terrorist forces the Navy repelled were invaders who meant every American, and all peoples everywhere, the greatest of harm. The Kresse was a great work of nature, but there was more at stake here than anyone could ever be allowed to know

"'This I believe.'"

Vincenzo came sober as if someone had thrown a switch. His smile disappearing up his sleeve, he narrowed his eyes and scanned me in a way I was getting used to. It reminded me of several days before, right after I had recorded the words I'd just read him from my copy of that day's transcripts. When he questioned my look and why I was reading to him, I told him that the biggest story of the year--my story--was a complete and utter fake, and then I told him what really happened.

I started by explaining my reaction.

I told him of Major Timothy Snowden of Naval Intelligence and his two vague government type

tag-alongs, how they eyed me at that moment, and how it made me feel as if my fate were being examined under their gaze like something in the hands of a praying mantis. It was a cold examination, being looked over so carefully, studied for a specific reason, calibrated for exactitude. If my sincerity had come up wanting, I did not want to know what would come next.

Oddly enough, with all I had at stake at that moment, I still found myself wondering how a male and female team could work together in covert situations these days without being nick-named Mulder and Scully by their compatriots. Of course, these two were nothing like their television counterparts. This pair had not been sent over by central casting; they were soldiers of the real government. They did dress neatly–in that one fact they did resembled the cartoon ways of Hollywood secret agents–but you also knew that was where such similarities ended–there would be no charming bickering, no ratings-grabbing, sexual-tension-charged disagreements between these two. They had been forged from the same bar of pig iron, possibly in the same mold.

Finally, after about three seconds which took several years to pass, I got the sense from where their expressions settled on their non-descript, government-issued faces that they believed me. That I would keep their secrets. For the same reasons they would. It was a rare moment, the military of

any government and the press agreeing on anything. With no coercion. No guns or threats. No–

"Anyway," I said, "that was the ending. That was the official statement the Navy requested for their records which, believe it or not, I was happy to give them. And so, now, Mr. Vincenzo, unless you are so under the influence of the grape that it is a waste of both our time, I am going to tell you what really happened. Are you interested in the sound of my voice, or not?"

Vincenzo nodded, buzzed for a bottle and several glasses to be brought in, and I proceeded to tell him what had been transpiring behind all the backs of everyone in the world since I had been sent from his offices the week previous out into a nightmare more bizarre, more insane than any I had ever previously known. It had, all in all, been one hell of a ride.

The whole thing had begun when a news story broke halfway up the California coastline unlike any other--at least, any other that had made the big time--national television news, that is. Which just goes to show what else might have happened for my career if ever I'd found the things I tend to find on a slow news day.

Piecing things together from the official police reports, it would be safe to say that on Saturday, August 15th, from roughly 6:45am until well into the afternoon of that same day, the police, first from the small seaport town of Rogers, California, and then those from their neighbor to the South, Pentella, had their hands full with one of their least favorite tasks--keeping the curious away from an actual mystery.

As usual, they did the standard things cops do, and they even recognized the fact that they really needed to keep people away from the site in this particular instance. But, even though most flights of Monday morning quarterbacking fancy are generally worthless exercises, all things considered I don't believe I can be blamed for thinking now that it was probably a good thing they didn't do a better job.

The constables of Rogers, officers Robert Dennis and Patricia Morten, were the first to respond to the 911 call of a dead man discovered on Pingle Beach. That the caller had been somewhat hysterical had not seemed noteworthy at first. Most people react badly to finding their first corpse, especially one that can only be identified as male because of its genitals.

It turned out that the particular stretch of Pingle sand, shells and seaweed in question was a cove where the Rogers town line met that of Pentella. Officers Dennis and Morten were quickly joined by their brother law enforcers from the neighboring jurisdiction.

Now, it must be noted that the quick arrival of the Pentella black & whites was not due to any kind of political turf war. Bodies wash up on beaches, even the pristine, Californian beaches all those wonderful songs were written about, with fair regularity. Folks missing off boats, surfers caught in the current, suicides–all manner of people die with their lungs filled with water and flecks of sea weed. But, there isn't a city council from Crescent City down to San Diego that wants anyone to think for even a moment that cold blue flesh ever washed up on any of their beachfront real estate.

Such ideas aren't good for business, you see, and most elected officials get elected to make certain things that weren't good for business do not occur. Or, at least, that they do not get noticed by anyone. But at approximately 10:45 on that same August the 15th, something happened that would throw more than a few local Californian politicians, and eventually the ones polishing chair seats in Sacramento, as well, into a frenzy that would last for some time.

With the arrival of the Rogers medical examiner at Pingle, a rare opportunity was handed to an enterprising freelance photographer, one Phillip Whitley. Phillip, a pasty, goggle-eyed man with thinning

hair and cigarette breath, was the kind of person not above diligently scanning the Pentella police communications to fish for leads. That morning, he found one.

Working quickly, he was able to get himself to the bay in question before the arrival of the Pentella examiner. Setting up his equipment on a bluff far above the beach where he was safely out of sight of the constables below, his entrepreneurial nature, coupled with some actual photographic expertise, allowed him the chance to use up most of four rolls of film.

The grand majority of his shots, of course, were useless–blurred, badly framed, showing far too little of what was intended and far too much of the medical examiner's arms and the firmly planted legs of lawmen instead. As any photojournalist can tell you, it is the price one is forced to pay when hurriedly snapping shots without anyone's permission.

Despite this handicap, however, there were a handful out of the ninety-three pictures Phillip snapped that afternoon which showed real promise. Clear, crisp, remarkable, and one that was simply unbelievable.

Truly unbelievable.

The shot that was sold to most agencies was still somewhat less than award-winning material, but it got across the essentials. Mainly, it revealed a hideously deformed body. A human body, yes, but one that seemed to be in not only a state of deterioration, but also one of transformation. After careful examination, the remains did prove to have been those of a human male at one time, but at the time of Phillip's shutter-bugging, they appeared to be half-way between still being human and almost being the fifties' most famous gillman.

It wasn't easy, but if you got out your magnifying glass, and you knew where to look, you could see more than a hint of gill development, the receding of the eye sockets, bulbous popping of the eyes, and other little details the trained observer could direct you toward. Of course, one had to allow for the added fact that this was a body which had been in the ocean for no little amount of time, soaking up salt water, bloating, wrinkling, turning first fish-white, then death-blue.

Its skin was stretched, and most of its hair missing. It was a disgusting thing to look at, chewed on and rotting, bloated and covered in sea weed and polyps--wide-eyes staring, mouth screaming open.

It was the kind of thing that in a gentler age nobody would have wanted to see.

At least, that's the lie we tell ourselves. The simple truth is, everyone wants to see every disgusting thing available. Don't believe me? Just get in your car and go driving for a while. Search out some heavily snarled traffic and then just get in line to see whatever it is everyone is gawking at. When you finally reach the front of the tangle, most of the time you won't even find an accident. No, most of the time you'll find that you've spent eighty minutes traveling five miles an hour so you can view someone getting a traffic ticket, or changing a flat.

The even simpler truth is that people are cowardly thrill-seekers, ever hoping to supplement their hollow existences with a bit of blood and damage sucked away vicariously from someone else's life.

Thus Mr. Whitley's hard work was plastered across the front pages of papers across the country, a fact that, when it first happened, had left my editor, the aforementioned Mr. Vincenzo, less than happy.

In fact, it was this less-than-happy soul who first showed me our colleague Whitley's delightful

bits of photo-journalism. Vincenzo was, at that first moment I saw him several days earlier, some-what upset with our own fine news force and the fact we had been upstaged by other papers. That good reporting had had nothing to do with their recent success had no bearing on the subject. Vincenzo has never been one to allow logic to interrupt a good rant.

"Have you seen this, Kolchak?"

"Seen what, Tony?" He thrust the paper in my hands, forcing the sun-washed photo in my face. Thumping the decaying corpse brutally with an extended finger, he shouted;

"This, this, this!

Haven't you seen this yet?"

"Tony," I responded, grabbing the paper from his hand, "have some respect. This is a newspaper, after all."

"A competitor's newspaper ..."

"Still, a thing deserving of respect. After all, you remember what Chesterton said about newspapers, don't you?"

"You mean," Vincenzo wrinkled his brow as he answered, "'Journalism consists largely in saying

"Lord Jones Dead," to people who never knew Lord Jones was alive.' Were those the thrilling words you were searching for, Carl?"

"Hummmmm," I answered as I studied the photo, "They could be, but I thought he had something nicer to say. But, what's the difference? Com'on now, Tony–spill. What is this? What's this all about?"

Vincenzo told me the whole story, what little he had been able to glean from the papers, the wire services, and those stations reporting on the discovery. As one might expect, the local jurisdictions upstate were not confirming anything for anybody. The gist of it, though–easy for any newsman to distill down out of the reams of mush being peddled—was that a male body in some state of distortion had washed up on a Californian beach. For whatever reason, the authorities were trying to keep a lid on things.

   End of story.

   "All right, so some guy died in the drink, soaked up enough salt water to distort his hide, and washed up again in the saintly small seaport town of Rogers, or its equally charming neighbor,

Pentella—take your pick." I held the paper out to Vincenzo the way one holds a Frisbee in front of a salivating Boston Terrier, "I ask again, so what?"

   "How can you stand there and give me 'so what?' You—Carl Kolchak? The king of the undead, the lord of the lizard people, viscount of the vampires ..."

   "Now you hold it right there, Vincenzo," I snapped. My transplanted Italian was getting ready to bombard me with his ire, and I was not having it. "I smell an attempt to make a point coming, one neither well-thought-out nor deserved. Are you trying to say that something here is my fault?"

"Yes, that's exactly what I'm saying. Ever since Vegas, every time you look behind a garbage can, there's Frankenstein's monster. Every time you peek down an alley, the Mole People come shambling out after you--"

"And every time you add too much wine to your tomato sauce the staff of the Hollywood Dispatch gets treated to either your rendition of the Beer Barrel Polka or one of your lunatic screaming fits, and frankly Vincenzo, to tell the truth, I am beginning to miss the accordion music."

"Now you listen to me, Kolchak. I'm not through with you on this. You got us both bounced out of

Las Vegas. Then I take pity on you up the coast and you get us both run down here to the Disgrace and, and ..."

I caught the fact that Vincenzo was so mad he had slipped and called our beloved "Dispatch" the "Disgrace" the way everyone else in town does. That told me a lot. It meant the pressures of trying to turn the slip-shod rag he had the dubious task of rebuilding were getting to him. As an editor-in-chief, he took an all-the-king's-horses kind of tumble when he fell down the well after me when I first encountered the darker side of reality.

Tony Vincenzo, when all the noise and smoke clears, is a good guy. Those aren't words I would say in his presence; he wouldn't want to hear them from anyone, and if I said them he'd just get embarrassed and have to start throwing things to cut the sentiment short. If he was acting this way, then my guess was the owner had gotten on him, leaving him no choice except to get on me.

Apparently it had been decided that for any other paper in the free world to have a gillman story before us was a crime against humanity–and that I was the public enemy #1 behind it. I tried to point out that I had filed plenty of stories like this one in the past–better ones–ones with murders attached, bloodied, beautiful women galore–but, it did no good, and I could understand why. This one had photographs. And one of them was really good.

Within forty-five minutes I was on my way upstate, with expense account money, no less. I wiled away the hours of staying just seven miles above the speed limit on Interstate 101 thinking of how many drinks I could order before I got back down to my own money. I'll admit that route might not have afforded the marvelous vista views of the Pacific that Highway 1 did, but at that time I was far more worried about speed than beauty. Besides, I'd seen water before–knew all about it. It's the stuff I told them not to bring on the side whenever I ordered a Scotch.

It was dark in Rogers by the time I finally pulled into town. I refer only to celestial lighting, however. The town itself, for possibly the first time since its incorporation in 1914, according to the rusting sign at its entrance, was ablaze, folks leaving lights on as if Californians could suddenly give away electricity. I moved my own pile of rusting metal through the streets with care, not daring to proceed over ten miles an hour for people were everywhere, and not being especially careful about their actions.

The inhabitants of Rogers seemed divided into several camps. Many seemed frightened out of their

wits. There were angry knots of men on street corners, waving their arms, talking about the end of the world, invaders from beyond, and I swear I heard the word "Atlantis" thrown in at least once. Others seemed to be taking the more traditional rout to being frightened, speaking in whispers, their wide eyes darting from spot to spot, necks hunched, backs tense. And, though their voices were being kept low, I swear I heard the word "Atlantis" at least once as I drove by those groups as well.

Then there were the free-wheelers, mostly younger citizens, as you might guess, those who considered the goings-on in town as some sort of carnival. They laughed and giggled as they ran through the loose crowds, pointing at different individuals and spots, then laughing further. They made me smile.

I was hoping that out of all the courses of action on public display that theirs would be the attitude that proved the wisest.

As I continued to soak in the local atmosphere, I began to realize the town was not nearly large enough to support the population wandering its streets. Upon finding the last free parking spot in Rogers, a few simply inquiries allowed me to confirm that most of the residents of Pentella had joined me there that night. It had somehow been decided that the body had ended in Rogers' jurisdiction, and thus if anything was going to be decided about the incident, those decisions would be made there.

Not wanting to miss out on being a part of the biggest thing to happen in the area since 1914, the residents of Pentella had been arriving in town all day–many had shown up the day before.

Of course, there were also others like myself there–plenty of us–but we were fairly easy to spot. Even those not chained to their news vans by lengths of cables, or being trailed by their camera and make-up people, stood out from the crowd. Yes, their costuming gave them away in many instances. But, more to the point, you could look at them and tell they were outsiders. They were not there to defend their homes, to be witness to a part of history, or just to do something more exciting on a Thursday night than feed like cows in front of their televisions.

No, they were on the job. They were on location, trying to find a way to utilize their expense vouchers at local diners and motels, desperately hoping that someone would indeed be forced to defend their homes. They were looking to be witnesses to a part of history, all right, but only so they could turn whatever monumental event might befall Rogers into simply more bovine fodder. Walking past those clusters, I heard the word "Atlantis" more times than I could count. Then, just when I was beginning to realize that things were spinning far out of control in formerly peaceful little Rogers, a voice stabbing outward from one of the busier knots of newshounds grabbed my attention.

"Carl, Carl Kolchak—you're here? All right, now I know it's the end of the world."

I turned, recognizing the voice of one Marvin Richards, host of the wildly popular show Challenge of the Unknown.

"What's your guess, Carl," he shouted as he made his way to me, "Creature from the Black Lagoon, or runaway resident of lost Atlantis?"

Richards was someone often mentioned in the same breath as myself. He was a newsman–yes–but where as I just can't seem to stop stumbling across the bizarre and the supernatural on a regular basis, Richards was in the business of making the bizarre, and especially the supernatural, the news of the moment.

"Tell your cameraman to kill his feed and I'll be happy to enlighten you, old scout."

Richards' smile exploded across his face. Giving the stringy twenty-something with the forty thousand dollars worth of equipment on his shoulder a hand motion that apparently meant "go wait somewhere else," the anchorman/producer turned to me and said;

"I have a trailer nearby where the Scotch is just the age you like it. Care to join me in a few?

"I will, indeed, kind sir," I told him, "But only after I offer you a touch of professional courtesy."

He tilted his head, indicating that he accepted. Giving him the best smile my Polish ancestry allowed, I told him, "I've got nothing, thus our entire time together will consist of me sucking down all the free info I can get along with those drinks."

Richards chuckled. Slapping me on the back gently, more to direct me toward his trailer rather than anything else, he started talking the second we began moving. As far as he was concerned, he still owed me one from the time I briefly worked for his show. What I did for him never made it onto the air, but he got enough material from me to produce a season's worth of dramatizations for Challenge of the Unknown. Complications lead to me not being paid anywhere near what I should have, so as Richards put it as he poured me a Scotch so smooth it made silk seem like gravel;

"Don't sweat it, Carl. Even by television standards you got a raw deal. What do you need?"

"Just enough runway to land on. I went out of town to a buddy's cabin for a couple of days, and ..."

"You?" The anchorman said the word with the same kind of shock one would upon discovering their lover was actually Osama Bin Laden. "I didn't think a nuclear war could get you out of sight of concrete and glass."

"Normally," I agreed. "But Chester keeps a nice bar, and on occasion I like to get away to pretend to be working on my book."

Richards laughed. I knew he wasn't laughing at me. There isn't an ink breather in the business who doesn't have half a manuscript moldering in a bottom drawer somewhere. Most of us drag it out at least once a year to celebrate our ability to kid ourselves that it will ever get finished. I actually edited a few of the old chapters this time, which meant I could ignore it for at least sixteen months now. Understanding completely, Richards topped off my drink and let me continue.

I told him that basically I had returned to town to find the gillman story on every headline and my editor barking for me to get an exclusive in twenty minutes or else. Thus I was there in Rogers

with less information than anyone else in town. As I told him;

"Because of some of the stories I've filed in the past, everyone just assumes that I've got some kind of hotline to Spook Central. And, of course, nothing I saw in the papers I had a chance to review said to me that there is necessarily anything supernatural going on up here."

Raising the curtain on the window next to me, I stared out at the citizens still milling in the street. Watching them move in their panicked circles, I let the curtain fall back into place.

"There's a lot of very scared people out there, but really, you must have all your ducks lined up by now. Do they have anything to worry about? Do you think there's anything to all this?"

"Don't know what to tell you, Carl. Here's what we have. If there's nothing going on, somebody should tell the government. The Pentella medical examiner signed off on the body, then went on vacation. The body was labeled a John Doe, and then the FBI swooped in and claimed it. Outside of Whitley's photos, nobody outside of those drawing paychecks signed by Uncle Sammy has seen a thing.

"The Navy is prowling the waters up and down the coast, but the claim is it's just scheduled maneuvers. My people have gotten statements with the cops that were at the scene, but everyone is oddly quiet."

Pressing a button, Richards called one of his people in, told them to make me hard copies of all the interviews they had done so far. When I thanked him, he said;

"Forget it—really. My exec producer has been after me to square things with you for months. I've left it off just to torture him. I knew you weren't the kind of guy to sue the company, but it never hurts to keep the suits off balance."

I toasted him with his own Scotch and told him what a truly magnificent gentlemen he was. He praised my ability to lie to someone's face, telling me that if I kept working at it someday I'd be as good at it as he was. I promised I'd study hard. Together we killed half a bottle, going over everything Richards' people could tell us.

Yes, there was a body. Yes, his people had studied the photos with their best equipment and from what they could tell, this was a one-of-a-kind corpse. As to what kind that was, however, he had no idea. We both made the point that the comparisons flying about to the "Creature from the Black Lagoon" film were silly, but not for the reason most would think.

The problem with the "reality" of the Creature film is, unlike that in the Wolfman, or Dracula, there wasn't supposed to be any supernatural element involved with that particular Universal Studio's beastie. The monster there was simply explained as being some kind of leftover from

another era, some kind of dinosaur or something. The problem with that is, was it supposed to be an immortal dinosaur? Because, if it wasn't, where was Mrs. Creature, and Grandpa Creature, and all the rest of the clan? Technically, even if you wanted to say it was the last of its kind, then still, where were at least the bones of a few of its predecessors?

I could certainly believe Whitley had been snapping pictures of the corpse of a water-breathing humanoid. Why not? I've seen everything else in my time. All things considered, the way things happen in my corner of the universe, I suppose it was probably time for fish-people to make an appearance. But, if that body from Pingle Beach actually was some kind of half-man, half-fish thing, then where were the rest of the fish people? Richards had no more ideas on that subject than I did, no matter how much of his Scotch we drank.

We brainstormed for a while longer, but nothing seemed to lead us anywhere. What we knew for sure was that the cops weren't talking beyond polite nothings, that the Navy was keeping the waters for nearly a hundred miles completely free of all traffic--maneuvers, you know, that the Pentella medical examiner had disappeared from public view, that no citizens had been allowed anywhere near the body--a body, curiously enough, which had gone from the beach straight into the hands of the FBI--and that Phillip Whitley had already given out the best of what he had.

We also knew that no one had the slightest idea from where the world's most celebrated corpse, of the moment, had come. There were a lot of theories, of course--there are always a bushelful of those available. But, when you came right down to it, because of the unusual currents in that area, the body could have been dumped right there on Pingle Beach, or it could have floated a mile from some other spot, or a thousand miles, and from most any direction. And, as for those who had seen it, the only voices describing the corpse, which no one further was being allowed to view, all said pretty much the same thing--that it was just a regular, average-sized Caucasian, or possible fair-skinned Latino, male, one simply somewhat distorted from its time in the water.

There was, of course, one person no one had heard from who could contradict these claims, the person who called the Rogers police force to tell them about the body in the first place. Early reports, before the lid had been clamped down on information, had described the caller as male--most likely older, retirement age. The call had been traced to a phone outside of a motel parking lot near the spot on the beach where the corpse was discovered. Or, in other words, someone who either did not own a cell phone, or did not want anyone to know who was calling, used the first phone they could

find to report what they had stumbled across. Questioning of the motel staff, their residents of recent and the motel's neighbors, had apparently so far brought no results.

I took two last favors from Marvin Richards-a half a club sandwich he had remaining from dinner, and a lead on an old woman on the outskirts of Rogers who might have a room to let. Actually, his people had grabbed it up along with a dozen others when they first got to town, scrambling to make certain they had enough beds for the entire crew. That one was left over, and he graciously donated it to the Dispatch's quest for truth and liberty.

"I'm going to extract a verbal contract from you, though, Carl, for our legal department," Richards told me. "This squares us up, right?"

I smiled, still holding three fingers of his Scotch in my hand. Flashing him a smile, I sipped one of them off the top, then held my hand up in a solemn salute while announcing, "Yes–this squares me with your production company."

Then, I knocked back the last two, flipped the glass through the air to its owner and told him, "You, you still owe me one."

Catching the tumbler cleanly, Richards held it at an angle as he asked, "Why's that?"

"Because I'm a greedy bastard, and you're just the poor, innocent little producer that I've leeched onto. I'm just lucky you feel sorry for me."

He smiled back, nodding as he agreed that he liked that assessment of our relationship. I thanked him for being so open-minded and then headed back to my car, hoping I could find 11 Broomewater St. and a Mrs. Gertrude Millsump who was to be my host for the next few days. Before I could reach my trusty vehicle, however, I was intercepted by two individuals who did not look much like citizens of either Rogers or Pentella, or media types, for that matter. They had the dedicated look of those on "official business;" not, as you might imagine, my favorite types in the world.

"Carl Kolchak?"

It was the female doing the barking. She was tall and sturdy enough to be commanding in most any circumstances. Her "show-me-respect-because-I'm-female" routine was fairly standard. I let her know how impressed I was.

"Very good scowl," I told her. "But that weak chin of yours undercuts it a bit. Perhaps if you wore higher collars, or perhaps if you let your beard grow in."

I saw a flash of light in her partner's eyes letting me know he was willing to try and sucker me with a "good cop" pose at any time. I smiled amiably at him as if I was suckered already. While we twinkled at each other, his partner snapped;

"I asked you a question, mister."

"Actually, my dear, you only said a name. Granted, you did allow a few notes of a questioning tone to mingle with that rusting muffler noise some charm school elocution teacher would find their greatest nightmare, but to ask a question, one needs–"

"You are Carl Kolchak, aren't you?"

"Hummmmm, half-question, half-declarative sentence. I believe you're getting the hang–"

"Listen, Kolchak–stop wasting everyone's time."

As I molded my features into their most innocent look, the snarling authority figure introduced herself as Linda Boll and her partner as Peter Norman, both of the FBI. She made some more noise in my direction, some about my attitude, some about how my presence was bound to make everything worse. I gave her a bit more guff, just because I was tired and felt like it. She threw a punch at my

head which she purposely turned at the last second. It only knocked my hat off but her point was taken.

Agent Norman, who seemed as if he spent a lot of time cleaning up after his partner's temper, caught my splendid chapeau in mid-air and returned it to me. His looked told me he was still amused with my antics, but that perhaps I should rein them in for the moment. I took his unspoken advice and allowed Ms. Boll to make a less awkward retreat. It dawned on me after I started on my way once more that things had gone so badly between myself and the FBI just then that I had no idea what they had wanted. I decided to count the incident as a victory and resume my hunt for the route to Broomewater and my new landlady.

L uckily, both proved easy enough to uncover. Upon my arrival, I found Mrs. Millsump an enthusiastic member of the public. Mostly confined to her home by her walker, she was eager for every scrap of news with which I could provide her. She listened to every word I had for her intently. You could see the wheels turning inside her head, evaluating each new idea.

We quickly ended up in the kitchen as she provided a never-ending buffet of left-overs and snacks--anything she could find to keep me talking. As every good freelancer knows, you never turn

down a free meal. Richards' half-sandwich was wrapped for the next day's lunch and I did most of the getting up and down to spare my hostess the pain of walking. We polished off the majority of her left-overs and all of her beers. When we got around to rehashing our theories for a second time, I told her maybe it was time I thought about hitting the sack. That was when she said;

"If I was thirty years younger, I'd be on that beach tomorrow morning with a shovel and a rake. If there was anything else worth finding, you believe me, I'd find it."

I believed her. And then, as I listened to her words in my head, and started to think "what if," I suddenly had an idea of my own. When I let her know what I was thinking, she smiled, then told me something else she'd try if she were thirty years younger. I asked her to wake me at six. She told me she'd have pancakes ready. By the time I settled into my bed, I was beginning to wish she was thirty years younger.

The next morning, filled with maple syrup, blueberries, buckwheat cakes and bacon, I headed for the beach to see if my one idea had any merit. The police presence had long retreated, but it had left traces of itself behind. Where the body had been found, a sea wall of sandbags had been erected and some 100 cubic yards of beach had been scooped up and removed. One might almost have blamed souvenir hunters, but the professional cuts and heavy-duty treads leading down to and away from the beach suggested that once the body had been spirited away, every bit of land around it for quite some ways had been taken as well.

My guess was the FBI. It wasn't that unusual, really. Police departments routinely had entire walls and ceilings removed from buildings if they decided they really had to have them both studied carefully and out of the hands of others. Considering the fact that the body they had could have been practically anything, from a visitor up from Atlantis or down from Venus, any crumb of DNA or anything else which might have scattered from the body was important, not only for the studying part, but for that keeping-out-of-the-hands-of-others part as well.

I was not there that morning to study sand, however. What I wanted was a look at those others who might be there to study sand. I picked a nice, comfortable-looking stretch of beach, kicked off my shoes, stuffed my socks inside them, and then just lounged, watching everyone that passed by with feigned disinterest. I was watching for someone in particular. Someone male. Someone older. Someone with regret in his eyes. It took roughly six and a half hours, but I finally found the fellow I was positive I was after.

He was at least in his sixties, more likely his seventies. He wore a frumpy white bag of a hat to keep the sun from toasting his hairless crown. He was clean shaven, and his clothing seemed relatively well-kept. Brushing sand off my own clothes, I threw my socks and shoes back on, hoping he wouldn't take off before I was ready for him. He didn't. Wandering over to him, I asked if I might borrow his cell phone. When he responded that he didn't own one, I said;

"That's what I figured. After all, if you owned one, you could have used it to call the police the other day, instead of having to go all the way to the motel." When he simply stared, I continued

calmly, "Oh, you remember, when you reported the body you found on the beach."

His look told me all I needed to know. He turned abruptly and began to march off, but I caught up to him easily. Though he tried to ignore me, I shouted at him;

"I figured you didn't have one, because if you did, then why make that long trek up the hill?"

He kept walking. I kept talking.

"The police reports said the caller was an older person, most definitely male." He threw himself into his forward motion, determined to shut me out. I felt sorry for him--slightly--the way one might a ladybug they accidentally swatted.

"They said the caller sounded agitated. More than worried. Frightened. Maybe terrified."

The man's pace slowed. I didn't think it had anything to do with his desires. He was simply an older man trying to make top speed while moving on sand. The two do not go well together—the harder one tries to race across sand, the harder such a journey generally tends to go.

"I wondered what would go through that a man's head. Especially when he saw the media circus growing up around such an event."

He slowed a bit more, possibly not so much this time out of age as out of curiosity.

"I mean, all those cameras and reporters, so many people around the world, interested in what was going on, and here this guy was ... the first person on the scene, and now he was too embarrassed to accept the credit for being that first person on the scene--for being the person who made not only the find of a lifetime, but maybe the discovery of the century."

The old man stopped. His shoulders shook a little as he made a half-hearted fist. It wasn't a thing of anger, but frustration. He wanted to be noticed, but he was ashamed.

"You didn't see it."

He said the words with his back to me, but I knew whom he was addressing. His shoulders crumbled, and he sunk in on himself. He had been defeated in his desire to escape. Not by me, but by himself.

"Please ... leave me alone."

There was a depth to the piteousness in his voice which would have brought a pope out of his marble tower to pray over him. I tried to make my voice its most reassuring.

"I only want to ask you a few questions; I just need to understand some–"

"You don't understand because you can't understand."

"Sir, please ..." I threw my own voice into a plea, begging him as he turned around with every syllable, "you're right. I can't understand anything where I don't have all the facts. But you ..."

I paused, grasping for words. I'd seen this reaction before. I'd looked into the eyes of a woman who had been kidnapped and tied down to be used–not for sex, but for producing blood. She had, for all intents and purposes, been turned into a cow to be milked for red blood cells, and the creature doing it thought less about its right to do so than we think of adding creme to our coffee. I'd looked into her eyes, and when he turned to me, I looked into his.

And this old man looked more frightened than she ever had.

He had not been harmed in any physical sense. He had not been abused, nor greatly interrupted in his daily routine. Again, not in any biologically injurious sense. But, he had been wounded, none the less. It was not flesh that had been tore within him, but his mind, instead. It had been assaulted by something it could not accept. The way a bullet presses against the flesh, trumping the ability of skin and sinew and bone to halt its progress--that was how his mind had been pummelled.

By an idea.

He had gazed upon the body there on the beach and he had seen something which officers Dennis and Morten had not. Nor their brothers of the badge from Pentella. Perhaps the Pentellan

ME had seen the same thing. Maybe he was not so much avoiding the media because of political considerations, but because he had seen the same possibility, some similar twist of logic which had frightened him to his core.

Just seeing the cold, etched horror in the witness's eyes had frozen me in my tracks for more seconds than I cared to admit. I couldn't help it, though; none of us can--our first time. When human beings encounter the strange, there's always that momentary brain freeze where our gears jam as we think about something we've just taken in, something so vastly different from the way things should be to us that the mere sight of it robs them of mobility until they can come to grips with it.

"Don't let it get to you," I told him. I did not anticipate his next reaction. The man suddenly fell forward into rage, hissing;

"What do you know about it? You don't know ... can't–you wouldn't be able to imagine it. It ..." As he gasped for breath, the slightest trickle of a tear squeezing free from his left eye, I whispered to him;

"You'd be surprised what I can imagine."

I said the words in just the right way to make him stop reacting to the entire world and focus in

on me. This time, instead of just throwing the look in his eyes at me as a warning, he stared past his own torment and tried to see me as a person. In some ways he liked what he saw, some made him more frightened than ever.

You have to understand, I'm not talking about some kind of mystic mind transfer here or anything. Anyone can do this. Think of any situation where there are a number of people in one place, but only you and one other person know something that the others do not. Just a quick glance into their eyes lets you know they share the knowledge you have. You can read it in their face. You don't know how you know, but you know you're right.

That's all that was happening here. As the old man stared into my eyes, he could see, not the things that I have seen, but the fact that I have seen them. He knew I understood that there were things beyond. The part of that he liked was that it meant he might not be crazy. The part that made him more frightened than ever was the fact that if he wasn't crazy, then what he was thinking he saw might actually be true. His hands shaking, he pointed one of them at me, asking in a whisper;

"Do you know ... what it was? Is? What's going on? How do you know ..."

I stopped him with an upheld hand. Motioning him toward me, I stepped toward him at the same

time. Putting out my hand, I took his and shook it as I said;

"My name is Carl Kolchak. I haven't seen any more of this gillman than most everyone else, but I have seen plenty of other things. Please, tell me what it is you saw. What is it that has you so spooked?"

We talked for several minutes. He introduced himself as Jeffrey Manders, but that was all the personal information he bothered with. He did not ask why I wanted to talk to him. Knowing that I could understand what he was feeling was all that mattered to my boy Jeffrey. I was someone else he could talk to--finally--about what had happened to him. He set about doing so immediately.

The first thing he described were its eyes. He called them bulbous, and said they were forward-staring, shifted from where they should be on the face out toward the sides of the head. It was, he admitted, not a tremendously great displacement, but it was enough to notice, enough to let him know he was in the presence of something wrong.

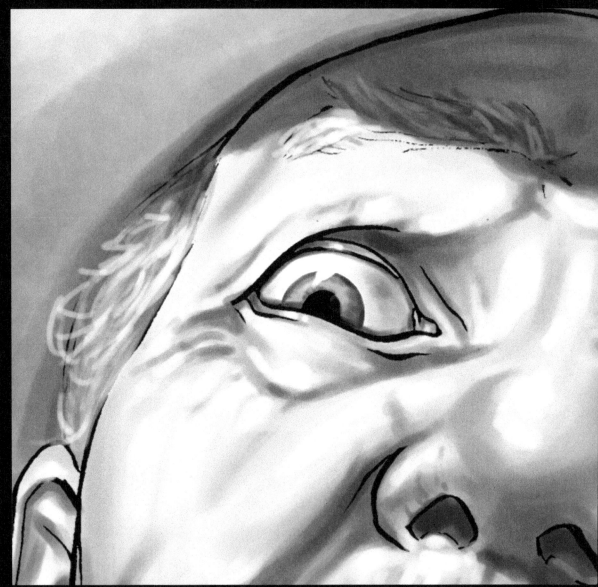

He also told me of touching the body, of how parts of it felt somewhat like normal skin, but how most of it had the feel of a fish.

"There were scales on my fingers after I touched it. Scales. Fish scales--they pulled away from the corpse and stuck to my hand. It was maddening. I mean, I thought I was losing my mind. It didn't make any sense, the way it just came crashing down onto the beach, I didn't know what to think, where it could have come from, lying there all crumpled--"

"Excuse me," I said, seconds after I actually wanted to do so. My new friend wasn't the only one who was a little startled. "What did you mean when you said ... 'came crashing down onto the beach?' I thought it had washed up from the ocean."

"Yes–of course, that's what everyone thinks–but ... they weren't there; they didn't see what I saw, didn't have to run from it–didn't have to ..."

Manders' voice had been growing louder with every other word, terror forcing him to practically scream by the time he abruptly stopped talking. A sea gull happened to glide overhead and its shadow sent the old man into spasms. At that point he let me know he was leaving. I could go with him if I wanted, but he had endured all of the beach he could for that afternoon. I, of course, accompanied him back to his home.

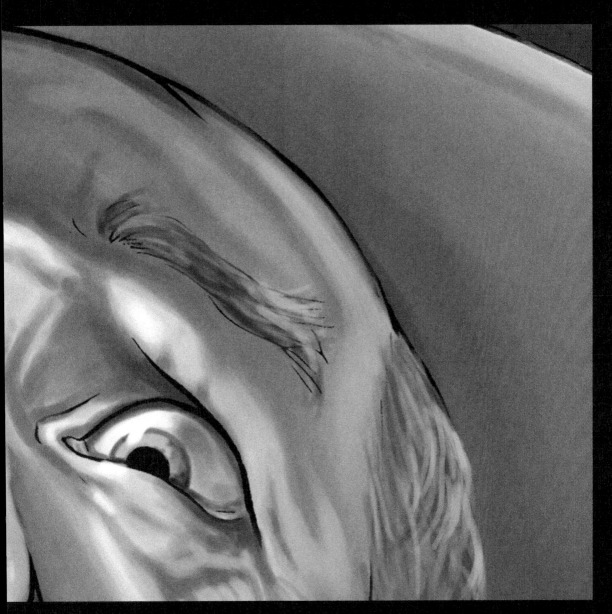

Manders was quiet throughout the drive. We shuffled into his modest one story home in the same silence, a quiet that was maintained while he pointed me to a seat and all the while he was preparing us a pot of tea. He returned to his living room with a tray containing a pair of mugs, a large ceramic tea pot and a plate of assorted cookies. Unable to contain himself any longer, however, he began telling his story once more while pouring. He had been walking the beach looking for shells as was his habit nearly every morning. When a large shadow raced along the beach he looked up, and noted what he thought at first to be a condor. It was struggling with something clasped in its talons, a struggle it lost at that moment. Its prize fell to the beach only yards from where Manders was standing.

The old man approached the body, had time enough to handle it, to note the gill slits, altered eyes, et cetera, and then before he knew it the thing that had dropped the body on the beach had arced back. By his best guess, Manders missed having his head torn loose by a fraction of a second.

"Now," I asked, "you said you thought it was a condor. Was it a condor?"

"No." The old man said the word quietly, but firmly, and with intense conviction. "I don't know what it was, but when it swooped down at me, when it chased me up the beach, I got too good a look at it. It wasn't no condor, wasn't no bird at all. If anything, it was a man."

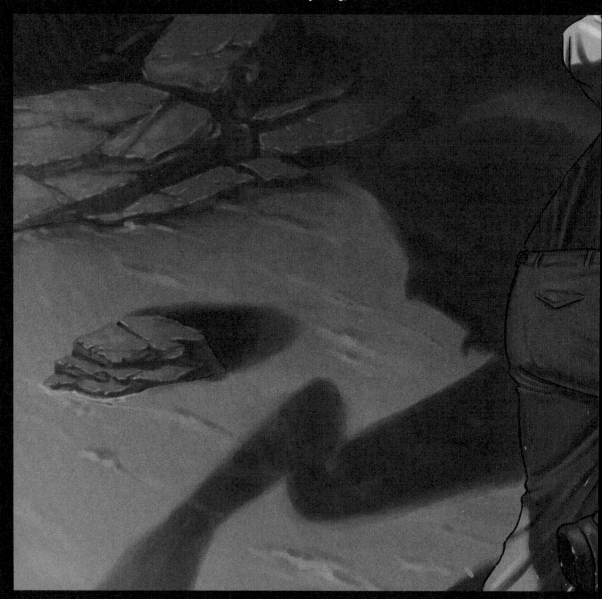

"Excuse me ..."

"You heard me. If that thing on the beach was a man of some kind, so was this thing. Its head was like a frog, or a lizard, a turtle, something–"

"I don't know what it was like exactly," he added, "but it was a man's face that had been twisted, like in a bad horror movie. It was covered in scales, too, but bigger ones, more plate-like. It didn't have a human mouth, but more of a beak, but one with animal teeth. And, of course, it had the wings– enormous wings. The span on them was, had to be ... I don't know, nine, ten, fifteen feet across."

"Feathered wings," I asked. "Like a bird's?"

"No. No feathers, no hair. Leather-like, stretched skin. That's the way it was, just scales all over its body. And horns, these two horns on its head, not so much like a cow's, like on a Viking helmet, but more like an insect's antenna."

Manders stopped talking abruptly. Picking up his mug of tea, he blew at the steam still rolling upward out of it, then gingerly sipped at the edge. I added a bit of lemon to mine then did the same. We sat in silence for a few long minutes, sipping, dunking cookies, avoiding talking. Finally, I asked him if he could remember anything else. He tittered a bit, then asked me;

"You want more? Isn't that enough? What more could you want?" I raised a hand to calm him, then answered;

"I'm just trying to put this whole thing together. If there's anything else you might remember, I'd want to know about it." I handed him one of my Dispatch cards, one of the ones I had scribbled Mrs. Millsump's phone number on, telling him I was ready to listen if he could think of anything else. I then thanked him for the tea and cookies, indicating that I had to be on my way. He nodded, then stopped me just as I was reaching for the doorknob.

"Mr. Kolchak, tell me ... you believe me. Don't you?"

"Yes, Mr. Manders," I assured him. "I can't prove anything you said, but I have no reason to think you're lying. You might be mistaken, but I've been around enough of these kinds of events to think you're not."

"Thank you," he answered. He wanted to say more, but there were tears in his voice, and he refused to allow what remained of his pride to take any more hits that day. I thanked him back for all his information. When he asked me what he should do, I told him honestly that he had two choices.

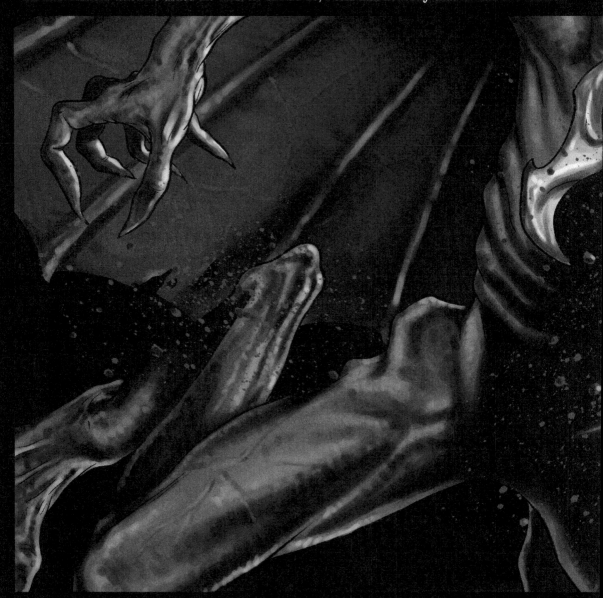

"You can tell people what you saw, or you can keep quiet. Most people will call you crazy if you talk, and you could quite possibly ruin your life. Yes, I'm a reporter, and you've just given me a leg up on everyone else—one that will be ruined if you tell other people what you told me. But, that's not why I said what I did."

He stared blankly, waiting for me to explain myself. I figured I owed it to him, so I said, "This is still America, Mr. Manders, you can talk to whomever you like. All I'm saying is that, in my time ... well, I've tried telling people about what I've seen, and it's only gotten me fired, laughed at, demoted, handcuffed, plopped down in front of psychiatrists and ridiculed."

"Then ..." he paused, gathered his courage, then asked, "why do you do it?"

"It's my job," I told him. Manders thought for just a moment as we stood there on his porch, then he smiled. Shaking my hand, he said;

"You tell whomever you want about it. I'll back you up if you send them to me, but myself ... well ... I think I'm going to stay inside for a few days."

His eyes glanced upward toward the sky. He made the gesture as a warning, one I took to heart. As I made my way down to the sidewalk, I noticed every time I looked back that he was still

watching the sky. Somehow, I didn't blame him. I'd done for him what Dr. Kirsten Helms had done for me; I'd laid a groundwork for him to handle his sanity-made the fantastic seem reasonable just through belief. It was the least I could do. He'd given me enough to take to the good doctor. Now, if she couldn't help me get a bit further ahead of the curve, I told myself, there would be no getting ahead at all.

I managed to make contact with her on the phone due to the hoopla in the media. I was right in the center of something I knew she wished she was young enough to still tackle with her own two hands. She'd been five years past retirement when I first met her. She was wizened now, but she still knew more than any encyclopedia and could cross-reference within her marvelous brain faster than any computer.

If there was something about the mythologies and superstitions of this event that she did not at least have a rudimentary knowledge of, it most likely wasn't worth knowing about. I told her every-

thing I knew and faxed her copies of all the transcripts I'd gotten from Marvin Richards.

For a long moment, she didn't say anything, which I found very intimidating. There are few women in this world who enjoy thrashing me with their superior knowledge of something more than Dr. Helms. The mere fact I still address her by her title after all the time I've known her ought to tell you something about her.

Eventually, after holding on for that long moment, leaving me to wonder if we'd been cut off, she finally admitted she had a quite positive idea about the corpse. After another, far brief pause, she added that she might have something about the winged things as well. The tone in her voice prompted me to ask;

"Dr. Helms, just a speculation, are these creatures, I don't know how to put it, ah ... related, in some manner?" After the briefest of pauses she asked for my address in Rogers, then told me to go out, have lunch and then call her back. That last moment of hesitation bothered me, simply because I'd never seen one in her before, let alone three in a row. And, if that caught my attention, the last thing she told me before she hung up really left me wondering.

"Carl," she said my name with a softness I had never heard in her voice no matter what the subject was, let alone me. If I'd had any way to understand what that tone implied, I don't know if I

would have lived out the week. "At lunch ... have something good. Something wonderful–something you really love."

"I'll do my best," I said in a perfunctory way. I was about to hang up, figuring we were just making end-of-conversation chatter, when the good doctor barked at me in the voice I knew best.

"You listen to me, Kolchak," she snarled, "if you like Chinese, go to the best Duck House in town and get the most wonderful meal they make. Spend whatever it takes to treat yourself to your favorites."

"Can I ask how important this is; or why I should do it?"

"Of course you can," she flung the words at me. "And if I told you why you should do it then there would be no point in the doing of it. So, just do it. If you need to, you'll understand later."

I rolled my eyes, wondering exactly what to make of her demand. Then suddenly, her voice softened again, and words came at me dressed in pity, composed from steel-girded compassion.

"You ... please ... just do it, Carl. Then call me when you're done. I'll have what you need."

Oh hell, all right, I thought. Why not?

I had a pocketful of Vincenzo's expense money, and luckily, what I like the best still isn't that expensive. Asking Mrs. Millsump's advice, I located the best Italian restaurant in the area and I headed there directly, inviting my landlady to join me. This was not a predatory invitation, you understand–she was, after all, a widow lady in her seventies. This was business.

She knew the area and she knew who lived in it. She had been a resident of Rogers her entire life. I pumped her until I knew all there was to know about everything in the area. Considering what little a woman of her age could eat, every tidbit I got was worth the price of her meal. It's sometimes difficult for an outsider to realize the importance of cultivating a locale. One never knows what they might learn about an area--or when that information might come in handy.

As for dinner, Mrs. Millsump had the linguini in clam sauce and a side of antipasto with a glass of red wine. I had the spaghetti, some fried calamari, and a heavy section of the bread basket. They had bread sticks with just the right amount of sesame seeds for my taste, something New York and Chicago understand, but which most of California does not. Normally I try to watch my bread intake, at least a little, but I couldn't shake Kirsten's admonishments, so I helped myself to all I wanted for

once, and then washed it down with as much beer as I could find. They had one of my favorites on tap, so I encouraged them to find a lot.

All in all, it was a meal well worth sitting down to.

By the time Mrs. Millsump and I had returned to the comfort and safety of #11 Broomewater, we had imbibed to the point where serenading the neighborhood with showtunes seemed like a good idea.

I was half way through what I thought was a stunning rendition of "If I Were A Rich Man" when a loud and singularly annoying voice, belonging to one Mr. Henry Bethel, my charming companion informed me, shattered the mood with an announcement. It seemed Mr. Bethel was quite the linguist, and was concerned with being able to hear every word of "Let's Make A Deal." Mrs. Millsump advanced the theory that Mr. Bethel was a "drip." I agreed with her heartily, and at that juncture we shook hands, then laughed and pointed at her loud and singularly annoying neighbor until he went inside #9 Broomewater. Declaring victory at the sight, we followed suit and went into #11.

When we reached the inside, I asked why my camera was sitting on top of her telephone. She stared at it as well, then answered that I had put it there to remind myself about something. I told her she was right, then set to scratching my head to see if I might be able to cut through the healthy amount of malt and hops blocking my memory of what that might be. The camera, by the way, was not some lunatic episode, but a trick I learned from my father. If you have something important to do and you're afraid you might forget to do it, place something out of order to jar your memory. It's a variation of the old tying a string around one's finger. Dad used to put a dining room chair up on the table. It looked odd, but whenever he entered the dining room, he always remembered what it was he was supposed to do pretty darn quick. And then he put the chair back down on the floor before Mother saw it.

Somehow, a stream of consciousness jolted from the image of my father hurrying to not displease my mother triggered my own memory. I, I snapped my fingers at the thought, was supposed to call Dr. Helms back as soon as I returned from lunch. Quite pleased with myself, I mentally thanked dear old Dad for another appointment successfully kept and started dialing the phone.

T he doctor answered on the first ring--halfway through it, actually--something I did not consider a good sign. Dr. Kirsten Helms is usually a quite busy woman. She is also old, and although she would never admit it, she is getting a bit slower. Even staggered as I was under the weight of so much good German brewing, I knew her speedy answer meant she had been sitting at the phone, waiting for me to call.

"Carl," her voice asked a touch shakily, "is that you?"

I went sober instantly. I could have had another pitcher. I could have had a keg. I could have been mainlining alcohol intravenously, and I would still have straightened out at the sound of her voice asking if it was me on the line. It meant she had been waiting for me to call. It meant that she was desperate about something–worried. It was a thing I did not believe possible. I had called her for information on vampires–vampires, for Christ's sake–and she treated it like a research question on the mating habits of the Canadian groundhog.

But now, suddenly the frosty, unflappable Kirsten Helms was frightened by something, and the

concept made my throat go dry. When I finally managed to croak out a response, she chastised me for being so slow. Our conversation did not improve any from there on.

Over the course of the next eighteen minutes, she told me a number of things. Some of them were direct facts. Others were websites she wanted me to check for myself. On top of that she told me she had already messengered several books to me that I could expect the next morning. Since it was completely out of character for her to simply volunteer information, I thanked her, then asked if everything was all right. She answered without hesitation.

"No, Carl, if any of this leads in the direction I fear, then no--not only is everything not all right, perhaps nothing is. I know I've made you work for your answers in the past, and ... God willing ... I'm looking forward to having more opportunities to do so again in the future. But for now, for right now--"

Her voice cracked and I did not know what to say. I had no comeback for the moment when the world's most self-assured and crotchety old lady broke like any one of the rest of us. She recovered her composure with a speed remarkable to behold, but I had been witness to the shattering of her

defenses, and the idea that it was possible overwhelmed me for a long, dry moment, like when you realize that there is no Santa Claus, or that your mother is just another mere and ordinary female. It was a world-view shattering moment, and it left me diminished.

"Kolchak," she finished, "you watch yourself. I've been looking into this one, and if it has any connection at all toward the direction I'm sending you, you could wind up so far in over your head that ..."

"Kirsten," I asked, more than slightly worried when she simply stopped talking, "are you all right?"

Her pause continued for a long moment–an uncomfortably long moment. Again, it was something acceptable in a normal person, but alarming coming from the good doctor. It meant she was uncertain, perhaps even fearful, and those were not building blocks one thought possible to find in the elemental chart of Dr. Kirsten Helms. Finally, though, she answered;

"No, Carl, I'm not all right. And I won't be until this whole business is over." There was another silence, and then she came back, telling me, "Like I said, if you need something, call. But don't just call to chat; I don't want to hear from you again until you can tell me this is over and done with."

I assured her I would do just that. Then, once our connection was broken, I got to work looking at everything she had given me–looking up the websites, coordinating the facts she had given me with what I could find on the internet.

I spent the rest of the day at it, skipping dinner and falling asleep at Mrs. Millsump's machine. When I awoke I discovered that the old dear had covered me with a handmade afghan. We had breakfast on the front porch, but we were glad when the Fed Ex truck arrived with the books Dr. Helms had sent me. That morning was unlike the day before's when I could sit on the beach barefoot for hours.

No, that morning, the sun had come out in full force, and there were barely any clouds to be seen, but somehow the day did not seem to want to warm up. There was a gray chill in the air, a cold dampness around the sky that made it appear as if one were viewing it through a light coating of gauze.

Inside, as I read the passages Dr. Helms had marked for me on the pages she had flagged, I began to feel a tightness drawing across my insides which I had not felt in a long time. What was developing within me, rather than the contentment one would expect from a plate of cheese-laden

scrambled eggs, a well-browned stack of sausage links, an equal weight of deliciously crisp hash browns and a quarter of a loaf of toast--buttered and jammed--was the beginning of a deep and shaky queasiness. I was beginning, for the first time in I could not say how long, to feel afraid.

No, "afraid" isn't a good enough word. We all feel fear--every day--it's what keeps us alive. Fear of pain keeps us from stepping off the curb into traffic; fear of abandonment makes us hold our tongue with lovers; fear of being unattractive keeps us from reaching for that second dessert. No, "afraid" was a trite and fragile binding to try and encompass what I was beginning to feel.

What I was beginning to feel was dread. Terror was creeping into my mind unbidden. After all I've seen in my time, I've managed to throw up some tremendously strong shields. I've put swamp monsters in their place, exorcised demons, taken down werewolves–I stopped a vampire, for God's sake. A vampire! Do you understand me? I, Carl Kolchak, one simple human being make of mere flesh and blood and propelled only by a cat-killing sense of journalistic curiosity kicked Dracula's ass. That counts for something. That gives a guy the right to feel like he's not just any average schmoe.

This whole thing, however, was taking me back to square one. Where I'd thought my education was fairly complete, that I knew pretty much all there was to know about monsters, it was beginning to look like my self-awarded masters degree was barely a grade school diploma.

I thought for a moment on the enormity of what it all might mean and I found my hands shaking, my groin shriveling, lips quivering. I sat for a while, simply staring, then shut all of Kirsten's books so their words couldn't stare back at me.

I managed to get a hold of myself after a while, but I could not help but notice that the day had gotten grayer, moister. More oppressive. Humid. Dank. Escaping weather like that was the only good thing about being fired years ago in New York. That was not the climate of the California coast. Something was wrong, and I had a terrible feeling I was standing in the center of it.

What was giving me that feeling was the picture Kirsten's various bits and pieces had formed for me. If folklore could be trusted, America had already had in its past as many sightings of fishmen as it had bigfoots. Much of it was rumor and urban legend, easily enough to dismiss, but much was not. There were, for instance, police reports out of New Orleans in the 1920s of tremendous battles–

both along the docks, and in town–with creatures similar to the one in Whitley's photo. The only difference is the reports described things in a much further state of evolution than what we had seen here in California.

And that was only one of scores of reports. The eastern coastline of North America was littered with them. The reason for this, more than one source felt, was due to sailing men out of New England bringing home artifacts and strange new ideas from their travels in the Pacific. One story out of that area in particular reflected our current situation ominously.

It took place close to a century previous–a seaport town in Massachusetts was raided by government agents. To the best anyone could discover, the residents were all taken into custody. None were given access to the courts. There were no trials, or even any records of charges being brought. But still, everyone in the town of Innsmouth was removed, and the entire place was leveled by explosives. There was talk of concentration camps, and dispersal to various naval and military prisons of those who survived the raids. The most disturbing similarity was the fact that the Navy was prowling the waters off the coast of Innsmouth, and that at the end of the government's

struggles with its citizens, submarines supposedly launched a score of torpedoes into the marine abyss below a reef offshore.

There were only a few theories about the origins of the creatures that held any water, and only one I was willing to give any credence. Dr. Helms had underlined one passage, writing "QUITE POSSIBLE" in the margin next to it.

If it was good enough for her, it was good enough for me. The idea put forth was that these things had at one time been normal human beings–that somehow an outside force had brought about this radical change. That made sense to me considering Whitley's model. There, as best anyone could tell, was a one-third fish, two-third's man creature. That sounds to me like someone who got interrupted while in the process of changing, not like something born that way.

The capper out of all I had read that morning, however, was a notice from New York City. It was dissimilar from most everything else Kirsten had put under my nose, but it was the most frightening bit of all. Everything else, you see, had involved fishmen. Most everything else she had sent took place early in the last century, with only hints and rumors about what might have happened since then.

This story, however, was current. It was the details concerning a recent firefight between

police and citizens struggling against monsters–monsters that entered a Manhattan restaurant and slaughtered customers until the police came. At that time they turned on the police and slaughtered them as well. After which, these leathery, scale covered things went out into the street and flew away. On wings with ten to fifteen foot wingspans.

This was all shortly before the terrible accident which destroyed the town of Elizabeth, NJ, and which obliterated a number of square miles of lower Manhattan.

I stared at the pages for a long time. Then I started drawing boxes on a legal pad, making lists and charts, diagraming the events I had before me. Before too long I had a time chart constructed which did nothing to relieve my uneasiness. It seemed the fishmen had first been spotted in this country in New England.

But in the nearly one hundred years since that time they had appeared up and down the coasts of both North and South America, as well as other spots around the world too numerous to mention.

Of course, it was all conjecture, all as much a myth as UFOs. Everyone had seen one, but no one had any proof. No one, that is, except Phillip Whitley. With his handful of photos, he had done what no one else had managed, he had breached the wall of doubt between those who would keep everyone in the dark, and public awareness of the world beyond. He was no crusader, no right-to-know fanatic--he was just a freelancer hustling a buck. But, he had blown the lid off a government conspiracy that went back almost a century, maybe more.

And worst of all, it was obviously still going on. The FBI had swooped in here just as they had done in this Innsmouth. The Navy was patrolling the waters off-shore once more, just as they had in 1928. And, I asked myself, what about these flying creatures? Were they mutants like the fishpeople? And, what kind of mutations were we talking about? And, was the cover-up of the fishmen extending to the fliers? Was the government covering up something about the New Jersey explosion where the flying things were seen before?

I must have presented a sorry picture, for Mrs. Millsump, hobbling by on her walker, stopped to cluck over me. She said I looked as if I had just received the worst news of my life. I told her I was probably just scaring myself. Then, before she could start the process of moving herself along, I asked her

"Tell me, this whole fishman thing. Does this remind you of anything else? Something from the past? I ask because, well, you've been living here all your life. Can you think back and tell me, do you remember anything like this at all--ever--anywhere around here?"

She scrunched up her brow, which brought all her wrinkles into play, making her face resemble a package of ground pork. You could see in the look in her eyes that she had some kind of an idea, but that she just couldn't remember it. I waited quietly, knowing that to interrupt such a memory

could chase it down a rathole forever. And then suddenly, she slapped her hands together and shouted;

"The Monastery. Oh, my goodness-how could I have forgotten the Monastery?"

"Well, Gertrude," I offered quietly, "I don't know how you could have forgotten the Monastery. Wha, what exactly is the Monastery?"

"'Course now," she admitted, "I can't say that it's related, but I remember when I was a little ; girl, oh my, we're talking back before the Stock Market crash, just a few years after the Great War ... I was maybe only five or six ..."

Mrs. Millsump slid herself into a chair, the escape from the strain of standing bringing a peace to the back of her eyes I hoped I would never need to understand. Relaxing, she fell into memory, and told me;

"My father and I had walked into town to do some sort of shopping. This was when I saw 'Froggy' for the first time. He was a strange-looking fellow; my father said he ran errands for the monks at the Monastery.

It wasn't really a religious place, not any more, he said. It had been, but then it had sort of fallen

into disrepair, and had just become a place for people who wanted to be left alone. Anyway, I've been puzzling over something in the back of my mind for days now, and that's it. That fellow on the beach, from the papers, he sort of had the same kind of look as Froggy."

It was not long before I was in my car and making my way a few miles up the coast to where the Monastery was supposed to be. My landlady's father had pointed out the road one took to it to her often, and she was able to remember several landmarks that should have made it easy for me to find. Remarkably, it took the rest of the day for me to uncover the place. Even though it was less than five miles up the road from Rogers, the Monastery had made no effort whatsoever to remain a part of the rest of the world.

There were no signs leading to it. Also, most of the landmarks Mrs. Millsump could remember had faded with time. Businesses had disappeared, a farm had turned into a golf course—the world changes as the decades roll along, including the world of the Monastery, which seemed to have fallen into decay. The road which led to it off from Highway #1 was slight and unassuming, overgrown to the point of almost achieving invisibility. Indeed, it became fairly obvious after I discovered it that it had suffered only foot traffic for some time.

As I navigated over the badly rutted trail, praying I would not leave too much of my vehicle along

the way, it dawned on me what this meant. If there were still people at the end of the road, they did not receive the services of any utilities. No gas trucks or electric company vehicles had been out to see them; no oil trucks, no parcel deliveries, no mail men--no, if the Monastery still had people living on its grounds, they would have to be totally self-sufficient. In this day and age, when folks can't seem to live without their cell phones, plasma televisions and I-Pods, I was not expecting to find much more than a few decaying buildings. As so often happens in this world, I was in for a surprise.

At the end of the road I found a gated fence, one chained and locked so long before the affair was now one large lump of rust holding everything tightly in place. Deciding my car was as safe there as it could be anywhere, I went over the fence where it seemed obvious from wear and tear that everyone else did who needed to either enter or leave the place.

Then, after some twenty minutes of pushing my way through knee-high weeds, I came to a clearing. What I saw beyond was definitely more than a handful of decaying buildings.

The Monastery, for all intents and purposes, seemed to be a going concern. The structures I could see from the tree line all seemed in reasonably good shape. The fields between myself and the buildings were well tended. And the place was by no means deserted. I could see folks performing normal farm tasks in every direction. Then the reverse became true and a number of them began to notice me.

My first instinct was to throw myself back into the woods but I killed the idea and held my ground. It was not bravery that prompted me, but more on the order of common sense. No one, after all, was pointing and screaming at the intrusion of an "outsider," which technically I certainly was. I was the trespasser here, and if the folks in the distance had something to hide, I had to assume they would be making far more of a fuss than they were.

As several of them started toward me, I decided to do what I had come for and started along an intercept course so I could meet them. After only about five minutes of both sides trying to bridge the gap between us did any of the residents draw close enough for me to begin to discern features. I must admit I did not take to what I saw approaching .

Those who lived at the resident were cut from the same cloth as Phil Whitley's Mr. X. Although

the degree of transformation ranged greatly from person to person, still the residents of the Monastery did seem to possess a great number of queerly narrow heads. Many of them shared the same type of oddly flat nose and bulgy, staring eyes. Most were bald or balding, including those members of the strange society who seemed to be female. If that last statement seems odd, just trust me when I say that I didn't want to stare, and I didn't want to ask. The lot of them also had the same overly wrinkled skin as that seen in Whitley's photo, rough and scabby, with the sides of their necks all shriveled or creased up.

"Hello, stranger," called one as they drew close enough.

"Hello, back," I answered, still smiling, still friendly.

"We don't get many visitors," the man called again. "Mainly because we don't particularly want any. Or didn't the lack of invitation catch your notice?"

The speaker's voice was even, perhaps a little tired, but not threatening. If anything, there was a note of resignation to his tone, as if he'd been waiting a long time for me, or someone, to come staggering through the brush.

"I did get the idea that you didn't get many visitors," I admitted. "But I didn't get the feeling we were unwelcome. If I was wrong, I could easily turn around."

"No," said the man in the lead. "That wouldn't be proper of us to chase you off, and it certainly wouldn't be the Christian thing to do. So, sir, if you'll follow me ..."

With that, I introduced myself, prompting the speaker to introduce himself as Luke Matthews. He told me that was the name he had taken when he'd rejected his "slave" name. Even with the freedom to be crass afforded we of the fourth estate, I was not certain how to ask him what he was talking about. Leaving off the fact that it was questionable as to whether or not there was any human blood in his veins, the flat white of his skin made it seem fairly certain there had never been any African blood there. When I finally professed my ignorance, he remained silent. Not wanting to be shown the gate, I changed tactics, asking;

"Forgive me. Let me just get to why I'm here out in the open. I just wanted to ask, have any of the men from your community gone missing of late?"

The group of them stopped in their tracks, all eyes focusing on me. The bulging, non-blinking

stares all around were unnerving, to say the least. Several of the group began to throw whispers back and forth between themselves, but Matthews put up his hand as a signal for such to cease. Shaking his bowed head back and forth slightly, he lifted his chin so that our eyes could meet, then gave me the slightest of grins.

"So, it's worse than I thought."

"What?" I asked him. "What's worse?"

"Follow me," Matthews said in that same resigned tone. He turned and started walking back toward the buildings. As everyone else turned and began following him back I thought, in for a penny..., and started after him myself. All along the way I saw more of the same kinds of folks, tending crops, clearing weeds, working at the thousand different chores every farm needs handled. When we reached the center of the compound, for lack of a better word, I was taken to a meeting hall type of structure. There Matthews and I got better acquainted.

He confirmed for me much of what Dr. Helms had sent, telling me of 18th and 19th century sea

captains, of their travels to the far East—and of what they brought back with them. They flooded their sea coast villages with golden artifacts—objects that came at a price. Town by town, these places became pockets of worship for unspeakable things. At first I thought he simply meant Satan. I've had enough run-ins with people who've turned their souls over to creatures fitting the Biblical descriptions of Lucifer to last me all of my days. But, he wasn't.

He was speaking of different things—older, more horrible, more terrifying things—things beyond imagination. The charm of the Bible comes from the fact that Beelzebub and his fellow critters actually care enough about us to want to see us turned from the eyes of God. But the elder things Matthews spoke of care nothing for us. They had no extremes of good and bad, no one to pray to, no ways to avoid destruction.

"You see," he said, drawing his history lesson to a conclusion, "out in the universe, the stars are aligning ... have been so for millennia. In the last few centuries, that alignment has been coming into focus–reaching completion, if you will. When the moment comes, when the gravities of the cosmos are in such proximity that the stage is set, then all the doorways will be opened at once, and these things will swarm in, unbidden, like pigs to the trough, and we all shall simply be so much garbage for them to consume."

I sat silent for a moment, then finally found my voice.

"Tell me," I said, "if these gods don't, ah, discriminate between those who have kept their faith and those who didn't, why bother to worship them? Was it just the gold?"

"No," Matthews responded. His single word drew some curious laughs from the others in the room. "Most men aren't that stupid. Our forefathers, the ones who pledged themselves to horrors like Gol-Goroth, Shub-Niggurath, Cthulhu, all the others, they knew they would be long dead before time came to pay the piper. For them, accepting the gold was just the teaser. What they were really after was the power that came with it."

M atthews painted me a picture of how those who prayed to these nightmares from beyond were rewarded with the transformation I could see in evidence around the room. His ancestors had been part of the Esoteric Order of Dagon and had given their adoration to this thing because they knew, did not believe, but knew, that if they did so they would be transformed, and that with that transformation came power.

"Once one of us goes completely over," he said slowly, "we become like a god on Earth. Deep Ones--that's the general term for a Dagonite who comes full term--they can breathe underwater, swim at

amazing speeds, withstand pressures unthinkable for a normal human. They can go down miles below the surface, then shoot straight back to sunlight without any fear of the bends. They're amazingly strong and long-lived as well.

"There are Deep Ones out there that are hundreds of years old. They know no disease; they do not infirm."

"When," I asked Matthews, "do they grow the wings?" And that one really stopped him cold. He stared at me for another long moment, then said;

"You're very good at your work, Mr. Kolchak. You seem to have put more of this together than anyone else. You're still off a bit, however. We here, as you might have begun to suspect, are not members of the Esoteric Order of Dagon. We are Christians. Not everyone, in what some two hundred years ago was know as the town of Balton's Crossing, fell in line with the Order. Obviously they did for a while, but along the way some of our great-grandfathers rejected the word of Dagon.

"Oh, it was quite clear the rewards were there for those who believed, but they were more worried about their souls than they were temporary mortal power, and so they returned to the flock,

and we have kept to their way of thinking ever since. We have remained on this one farm, all that survives Balton's Crossing, hidden from the eyes of man. We pay our taxes–there is still quite a lot of gold on hand, and we see passing it on to the government as just taking it from one evil set of hands and dropping it into another."

I was beginning to take quite a liking to poor, sad Luke Matthews. He was a decent, God-fearing man who knew there were horrors in the universe, and who had made a conscious decision to put his faith and trust and future in the hands of his personal choice for savior—Jesus—a popular choice, to be certain. He told me that with each generation of their small group which stayed the course, the effects of their great-grandfathers' blasphemies reversed itself a bit further.

And then, when all was said and done and we had cleared all the background material up, that was

when he explained to me how one of their citizens had ended up on Pingle Beach, and how men grew wings.

An hour later I was back at the fence surrounding the farm. I said goodbye to my small escort, letting them know I would do my best to keep them out of the papers. With all the other information they had given me, a farmload of Jesus-happy gillboys and girls wasn't going to get anyone too excited.

By the time I slid behind the wheel of my car I was fairly pleased with myself. There was something about Matthews and the rest of his bunch that made me trust them. They had turned their backs on wealth, power and all the other traps of civilization to live out their days quietly. I knew that with all they had told me that I was now sitting on top of the biggest story of the century. In fact, so much had gone so right so quickly that I was in no way, shape or form prepared for what occurred next.

I slid my key into the ignition lock, turned it, and nothing happened. I turned it again, and then again, receiving nothing more for my troubles than a sharp clicking sound. This worried me to no end–my mind covering light years in seconds. Had I misread the Balton's Crossing bunch? Had one of them sabotaged my car? Had I been set-up to be on the receiving end of some of their sharp-clawed grandpappies?

None of that made sense, of course. Why take me down into their home if they were only going to do that? Then again, maybe they were legit, but their Deep One ancestors were keeping an eye on them. Maybe eliminating outside influences was something they considered a familial duty. I heard a slight noise in the brush and my heart throbbed loud enough for me to hear it through my chest.

Instantly my mind flashed across every cheap horror film I had ever seen. It's just a cat, I told myself, or maybe a raccoon or deer or possum or something else that belongs in the forest. I stared out through the windshield, looking for some sign of movement, for anything that would let me know I was about to be swallowed whole by some kind of nightmare beast. Then, I turned to the left and stared out my driver's side window. I waved weakly at the sight of FBI agent Linda Boll.

"Oh, hi," I said, waving to her weakly. "I was just thinking of you."

It had been Boll and Norman who had crippled my car, or to be more specific, a Marine escort working with them. While their efficient-looking killer undisabled my fragile transportation system, his keepers slid into my car with me, Norman in the front seat, Boll in the back. Just for fun someone I didn't know went in along with her. He introduced himself, saying;

"Hello, Mr. Kolchak; I'm Major Timothy Snowden, Naval Intelligence. I'd appreciate it greatly if

you'd tell us everything you learned in there." I made an attempt to protest, but the major put up his hand and added, "And in return for such cooperation, the government would show their appreciation by telling you everything they know about this affair."

I have to admit, for once in my long and less than illustrious career, I had nothing to say. As immediately tempting as the offer was, it smacked of being far too good to be true. When I told Snowden so, he agreed that was exactly how it sounded. He also added a bit more.

"Let me be perfectly frank, sir. I'm willing to bet that part of what you were told in there involved the concept of the end of the world. Mr. Kolchak, it's time for everyone to put their cards on the table and if they don't do it as fast as possible we might all be looking back at this moment wishing it had gone differently.

"In other words, with the very real and possible thought that there might not be any tomorrow for any of us, I'm not concerned about giving you facts for a news story that might never see the light of day mainly because the light of day might soon get sucked down into the ninth ring of Hell."

I nodded to the major. He did have a point. Rolling his offer around in my head for a moment, I finally said;

"All in all, not a bad offer. Anywhere in particular you'd like to go to talk it over? We could take my car."

Snowden smiled. It was not the smug sneer of a typical Hollywood-style government lackey, but a far more sincere gesture. He had simply liked my little joke. It was a small thing, but it made me feel right in trusting him. He told me just to get back out on the main road and head south. When I asked if they had been following me all along, Boll chirped in;

"Until you stumbled across Balton's Crossing you weren't that important. Once we realized you were heading this way we decided to see what you could learn."

"How did you know I had learned about the Monastery?"

"We didn't," responded Norman. "But when we saw where you were headed ..." the funny glance I gave him forced him to admit, "when I returned your hat to you in Rogers, I had slipped a transmitter into the sweat band. Too compact for us to receive audio, but at the time we didn't think we'd need that–just wanted to know where you were."

"My tax dollars at work, eh?" Noises of agreement came from the various government representatives to whom I was playing cabby as we made our merry way back down to Rogers. Or, more specifically, a mobile command center the Navy had set up outside of the town.

On the way there we managed to cover a lot of ground. They filled me in on what the government knew of the happy Christian gillfolk, which basically tallied with what they had told me themselves. We all agreed Matthews and his bunch were no threat to the country or anyone else. I told them every-thing I'd been told up to the point where I'd asked how a Deep One earned his wings. It did not surprise me all that much that the Navy and the FBI were aware of the winged nightmares. It did surprise them that I knew about them, however. When I dropped the bombshell of the body on the beach being deposited there from the sky, I surprised them further.

"How the goddamned hell did you know that?"

The evident shock in Boll's voice did much to sooth my ego after the ease with which she and her deceptively friendly partner had planted their bug on me. I did not drop a dime on Manders, but I did explain enough to satisfy them. By this time we had reached their base of operations and it had been deemed necessary to stop talking about anything sensitive until we had crossed the parking lot

and reached a secure building. Once inside, with coffees all around, I let fall my next surprise.

"The last thing I have to tell you involves these Gol-Gorathians. Matthews was fairly positive that his missing farmer had been murdered by them."

"Why's that?" snapped Boll.

"Because they, the farmers, I mean, are being harassed by their flying cousins; they want the farmers to fall in line, go back to the old ways–join the winning side. Seems that some big moment is approaching or somethi–"

I did not get to finish my statement. All three of my companions interrupted me, Boll to scream for an aide-de-camp, Norman to tell me to hold on a minute and Snowden to slam his fist into his palm while he announced to the room in general that he "knew it!" The meeting room became a bedlam of activity as orders were given for this and that person to be found immediately. Every time I tried to speak I was told to wait until everyone necessary was present. Admitting that I could see the wisdom in that, I shut up and waited. It only took a few minutes these various "others" to be located and hustled in to join us. Introductions were made hastily and then I was asked to continue.

"Like I said, the fliers wanted the farmers to continue their transformations. They refused."

"I told you," said a professor Zachery Goward, the only other civilian in the room. He was tall, with intently blazing blue eyes and a thin frame, both from a hyperbolic metabolism and small bone structure. He was also square-shouldered and filled with energy, his voice flush with enthusiasm as he announced, "They were behind the destruction in Jersey and Manhattan, and they're behind what's been happening here."

"What's been happening here?"

My question brought the speaker's attention squarely on me. His voice was a gruff instrument and from the way he beat people with it I got the feeling he was an academic used to lecturing without having to defend himself often–sort of the world of education's answer to Tony Vincenzo. He shot a glance over to Snowden, got a signal from him that it was all right to share information with me, and started unloading;

"The Golgors, the fliers, as you call them, they are a much more recent addition to the catalogue

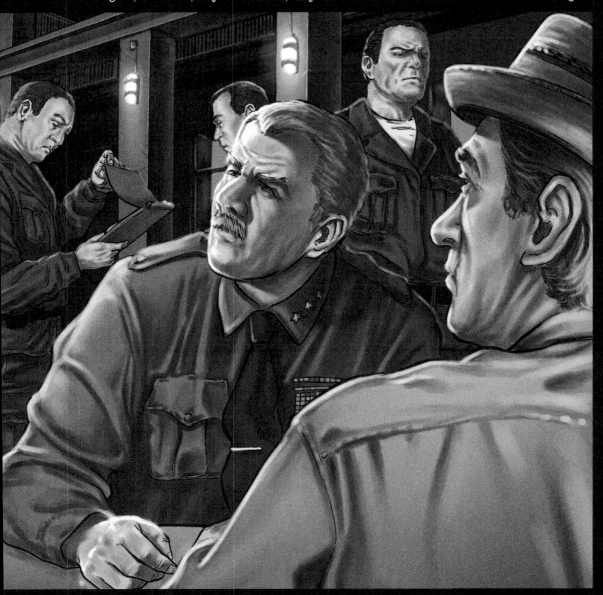

of nightbumpers. Mr. Kolchak, you're a reporter–yes? The one who's had such an interesting string of cases over the past several years?" I gave him a nod admitting I was that interesting fellow.

"Right then, you know what I mean. You're used to the simple horrors, the tiny frights like vampires and witches, demons, werewolves, zombies–there are the kinds of things you've stumbled over–correct?"

"Well, it's not like I keep them underfoot in my bedroom," I said somewhat defensively, "but yeah, isn't that enough? You ever find yourself trapped on a ocean liner with a 'simple horror' like a werewolf? You find out how very little room there is on one of those boats when something that can tear metal hinges apart is following you from deck to deck."

"Not my point, sir. What I'm trying to say is that we're dealing with something now that is larger than your frame of reference. What we're after now, is as far removed from what you know to be true as what you know is removed from what the average man in the street knows to be true."

I thought about what he was saying for a moment. People were still slamming about the room, jabbering into phones, typing away at computers, referring to maps, consulting star charts. It was a mob scene straight out of a sci fi movie, and I was wondering what the hell I was doing there. In that split-second, what Goward had said rang crystal clear to me. And suddenly, in an epiphany where everything came crashing together for me, I said;

"You don't know where the Golgors are, do you?"

Heads turned toward me as if I were a cheerleader who had just thrown all her clothes in the air. Instantly Snowden barked;

"Where are they?"

Again I liked the man. He did not doubt; he did not question how I could know, but simply what I knew. I told him.

"They're in the Kresse Caverns."

The Kresse Caverns are an unusual local phenomenon, a set of crystalline caves which open onto the shoreline. Most of the day the entrance to them is underwater. There is only a brief period when the tide recedes long enough for anyone to enter, and even then only the smallest of crafts can make

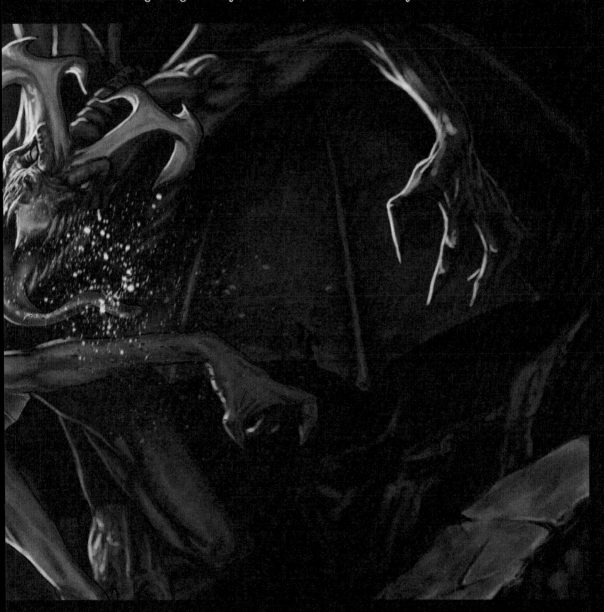

it inside. After scuba divers made there way inside some fifty years ago, the government deemed the entire area part of the national parks program and greatly restricted access to it.

"That's absurd," snapped Boll. "We've already had it checked. Our teams found nothing."

"What do you want from me," I asked. "One of the farmers swam in there to tell the Golgors the Monastery didn't want any part of them. He never came back."

"We didn't do an extensive search," Snowden admitted nervously. "We've been trying to cover the entire coast. There's no way our people could enter that place without it being known by the Golgors."

"They're excellent hiders," Goward chimed in. "Some believe they have the ability to merge with the shadows."

"No place has more shadows that a cave where the sun don't shine," Norman added. "All those things would have to do is avoid our people's lights."

"What'd you send in," I asked. "Two small launches, each holding a few marines, a flashlight in one hand, checklist in another. Drive around, see nothing, on to the next site. Is that how it went?"

I looked into Snowden's eyes and beheld a level of torture I could not gauge. There was something

I still did not understand, some last fact spinning just outside my grasp. I turned to professor Goward and asked in a whisper;

"What's everyone so tense about? Isn't this a good thing? You just go in, do a better check, they'll be all bottled up in there. Isn't it—"

He cut me off. Motioning me to follow him, he walked toward the wall, questioning me as we went.

"Do you believe the end of the world is possible, Mr. Kolchak?"

"Well, I ..."

"Yes, most of us don't like to think about it. But, mankind has known it was coming for some time now. We've postponed it more than once. A few months ago, back East, when Elizabeth, New Jersey disappeared in smoke and thunder, it almost came then. Now it's starting again." Pulling back the heavy curtain over the closest window slightly, he pointed outside and asked;

"Does that look like a typical Californian day to you, sir?"

It didn't. California got rainy days and gray days like anywhere else--not often, of course, but it got them. But, the sky on the other side of the window didn't threaten a shower. There was a strange depth to the darkening color it held, a repulsive scum in its tone that promised something

... something irrational, maddening, beyond human comprehension. As I simply stared, he quoted;

"'Brief and powerless is Man's life; on him and all his race the slow, sure doom falls pitiless and dark."

"Stan Lee?" I asked, only half joking.

"Bertrand Russell," he informed me, then added, "Mankind is running out of time once more, Mr. Kolchak. Indeed, the game is actually over--has been for some years. We're simply trying to gain humanity another overtime."

Across the room, men were shouting, laying maps one over the other. It seemed much of Pentella stood atop a large portion of the Kresse. Snowden counted off a handful of seconds in his head, then started barking orders;

"Okay, everyone—let's do this. Professor, do we even have a day left? Just one full day?" Goward pursed his lips, then shrugged his shoulders in response.

"Good enough. I hereby officially take responsibility for anything that comes next. Jensen—mobile

Charlie Team, get Operation Cleansweep moving. I want Pentella empty in ninety minutes. Ninety! Got it?"

The details are simple. The Navy had been ready for days to evacuate any area along the coast they had to. With half the residents of Pentella already staying in Rogers, their plan went off without a snag. A tanker truck was driven into the center of town and crashed into a van. A prearranged leak of harmless vapor was begun, labeled by the driver of the truck as a deadly menace to all human life—instantly fatal. A convenient cadre of military police volunteered to help clear the town. In less than fifty minutes, Major Snowden had his ghost town.

He sat in the command room in the last minutes before the end and simply stared at the activity all around him. Turning to me, he said with a laugh;

"It's funny, you know. We had our data, had checked out the Monastery thoroughly. We knew they were no threat. Oh, we had a watch on them, just in case, but ... we never ... I mean, it was all so ... I ..."

I didn't know what to say. I understood what the major was feeling only in the fact that I was feeling the same thing. Most people don't believe in monsters. Science has pushed all that nonsense out the window for them. Such thinking makes it all the harder for those who do run up

against, as Goward called them, the "simple horrors," the "tiny frights," vampires and witches, demons, werewolves, zombies–all the kinds of things I've stumbled over. Each encounter prepares one for the next, but still, each of them is the same kind of lesson. You learn there really are things that go bump in the night. After a while you can get kind of smug about it.

But this, this was different. This was a new lesson. This was not a single monster, this was scores of them. Billions of them. This was all of us, every yapping human mouth as a possible nightmare from above, each new greedy bastard helping to hurry the last moments of light and sanity. I looked to Goward as this thought came clear in my head. Outside, a stalk of lightning shattered against the ground in the distance. Seconds later, a thick rain began lashing against the window.

Across the room, Snowden stared at the glass, listened to the dark water slamming against it, then asked;

"Do the ships have their target coordinates?"

When that was confirmed, he asked;

"All landing craft ready? Scuba teams? Submarine squads? Sweep teams?"

All his questions were answered in the positive. Still, the man paused. He was about to set Armageddon into motion. On a hunch. Worse, I thought, on a hunch he'd formed from information

I'd given him. If I had read Luke Matthews and his people wrong, if I'd been suckered ...

Another slash of lightning illuminate the black torrent crashing down out of the sky, punctuating Snowden's order:

"Drop the nets and commence firing."

Seconds later, even as a fleet of small vessels began deploying several miles of industrial strength netting, from seven spots along the California coast a staggering collection of rockets, missiles and massive shells were sent speeding toward the Kresse Caverns and the town of Pentella. For some fifteen minutes hundreds of thousands of pounds of explosives devastated the village and the caves below. A small fleet of submarines converged on the area as well, sending waves of torpedoes in, blasting the coastline, toppling ton after ton of cliffside into the ocean.

Despite the driving storm, a thousand fires raged over several miles of countryside. The continual bombing would snuff some of the flames, only to set other areas ablaze. Then, when the shelling was brought to a halt, before the columns of smoke could even begin to be dissolved by the lashing rain, several dozen landing crafts jammed with marines were sent in to kill anything they might find moving. They knew what their enemy was. Had been shown pictures, been given

descriptions, told endlessly of their targets' inhuman natures. It was not enough. After he gave the order for his troops to be sent in, Snowden stood up as aides strapped a brace of pistols around his waste, put a helmet on his head, slid a military slicker over his shoulders. When I questioned what he was doing, he said;

"Mr. Kolchak, you see a major commanding this operation because no admiral wanted the assignment. I just leveled an American town and a national treasure. I just sent some two thousand marines into harm's way. If I was wrong, you're looking at a man with nothing to lose. If I was right, however, I'd like to see what I was so goddamned right about."

I saw his point. As he brushed away the aide trying to button his overcoat, he added; "You coming, Kolchak?"

I followed him out into the rain. We boarded his personal transport and were on the scene in less than fifteen minutes. What we found was more than horrible, or simply staggering. It was nightmare. Everywhere we went we saw troops battling for their lives.

From every water source, through cracks in the ground, up out of the sewers came fully

transformed Deep Ones--hideous, hard-scale covered monsters with wicked fangs and terrible claws which attacked with a vicious ferocity. Their skin was resistant to much small arms fire and it was evident that they tore their way through much of the first line of troops with ease.

The bodies of soldiers lie everywhere, crumpled, torn apart, eviscerated. Their limbs were broken; their eyes bulged in terror. Then, a score of yards into the combat, the bodies of Deep Ones began to be found, as well as Golgors. The monsters bled like anything else. Their bones shattered, their brains could be spilled. The rain pelted our bodies, slammed against our faces, and mingled with the various colored bloods soaking into the ground.

It was only the middle of the afternoon, but the sky was as black as a moonless night. The Deep Ones were already finished, repelled back into the sea where the majority of them were swept up in the killer whale nets that awaited them. They would, reports would tell Snowden later, climb the nets and engage the troops aboard ship. That move had been anticipated. The combat was supposedly horrendous. Few were captured alive.

Golgors swooped in on the marines in the remains of Pentella, tearing their heads off, slashing their throats, lifting them high into the air and dropping them from dizzying heights. They were hard to spot in the rain, an element they moved through as easily as air, despite the fact it was far too brutal to allow helicopter travel.

I stood with Snowden when he stopped and I walked with him when he walked. It was not something I did out of respect, or fear. Truthfully, I didn't even notice it happening at the time. I simply needed something to mark myself against, and the major was as useful a tool as anything else.

ventually Goward was brought to the area. He was escorted by a support team numbering over one hundred men-at-arms down into the remains of the Kresse. By the time the battle ended, the storm had dissipated completely. Sunlight streamed into the ruins of the caverns, reflecting off the millions of suddenly revealed crystalline facets. Snowden and I followed them down. What we found in the furthest recesses of the caverns was an altar carved into the ceiling.

Goward consulted several old books that had been brought in wrapped in protective layers of plastic, set inside locked metal boxes. The plastic was a safeguard against the rain. The metal boxes

and the locks, I don't want to speculate on what those were safeguards against. I recognized one of the books from back when I had briefly worked with Marvin Richards. It was called the Necronomicon, and I shuddered involuntarily at the sight of it. After checking several points in each of the tomes, the professor guaranteed that they had stopped whatever the Golgors had been up to in time. Our collective sigh of relief could have extinguished a bonfire.

We made our way back to the Navy's temporary base outside of Rogers. We were tired--exhausted, really--covered with muck and blood and bits of shredded flesh. Food was distributed, but no one really ate. There wasn't a one of us that shouldn't have been hungry, but it was as if food didn't matter.

What was the point of eating, I heard the back of my mind query. It only kept you alive longer. At the time, I had no arguments.

Then came the moment I had been expecting, but for totally different reasons. With an effort to match that of Sisyphus, Major Snowden turned to me and asked if I would consider not telling the truth of what had happened that day. Letting my indignation run on auto-pilot, I heard myself shout;

"Brother, isn't this always the case. And I trusted you–I really trusted you. Son of a bitch--why did you bother letting me go out there if you were to snatch it all away from me? What the--"

Professor Goward put up a hand to interrupt me. As I wheeled on him, he explained himself.

"Mr. Kolchak, there is a danger here that I'm certain you would realize for yourself in time, but allow me to 'cut to the chase,' as they say. We live in the most dangerous era mankind has ever known. As long as the heavens are still in adjustment, the end of the world is something that will be--every moment of every day--just around the corner. Any group of madmen or cultists, with but a few incantations, will be able to throw open the doors to Ragnarök."

"But what's your point, professor? Shouldn't we be letting people know what's coming? How can anyone help us avoid the falling of your 'slow, sure doom' if they don't know what's coming?"

"To convince people of the truth we know, we would have to reveal to them all the facts, including the most dangerous one of all, the fact that tremendous personal wealth and power is available to all who will submit to the power of the old ones. Think on that fact for a moment, if you will."

I did. I didn't like the conclusions I found myself drawing. If we did tell the world what happened, how long would it be before every reject loser in every corner of the globe was praying to the darkness,

begging for gold and super strength, for the ability to live forever underwater, or in the clouds? How long before the number of Deep Ones in the seas was in the millions? Or billions?

It was, to say the least, a disturbing thought. An unimaginable one.

The government did not leave me empty-handed, of course. They needed a cover story, and having a rabid, underdog reporter on hand to tell the world "what really happened" was, well, just perfect for them. And so the evidence was manufactured and my story went out--terrorists take over town of Pentella so they can reach the Kresse unobserved.

Their reason–to set off a nuclear bomb that they hoped would drop California into the ocean. The caves of the Kresse extended far inland. It was absurd, but we had the bodies, the bomb was easy enough to produce, and with Carl Kolchak to guarantee the story's authenticity, well, who could doubt it?

No one did.

As I finished my tale, Vincenzo looked as sober as anyone had ever seen him, including his first grade teacher. Over the next few weeks, we capitalized on the story for the good of the Dispatch,

but turned down personal gain. We did not petition the Pulitzer committee. I did not take any of the hundreds of offers to appear on television, or to relocate to other papers. It would have been taking false honors, and of late I've been thinking that keeping one's soul polished is a full time job.

I'm also hoping that if I put enough effort in that direction that someday I'll be able to start feeling safe once more–less threatened by the future Snowden and Goward feel is so inevitably hangin over us. Being convinced the end of the world is as tangible a concept as the new fall line-up, a lot of things begin to lose their importance.

Kirsten had been right.

I thanked her when I called her to tell her everything was over–for now. Even though right now every meal seems to have the same dull, zestless flavor, the effort I put into enjoying my lunch with Mrs. Millsump has stayed with me. I can still taste the richness of the sauce, the gusty savor of the meatballs–washed down by buckets of the world's best beer. Though now everything tastes like a

waste of time, I can remember that meal clearly, and it gives me hope that someday the sight of a simple basket of breadsticks, covered in enough sesame seeds to die for, will suddenly be a thing of wonder once more.

I don't have great hopes, but I have some. I guess that'll have to be enough.

KOLCHAK:™
The Night Stalker
the LOVECRAFTIAN
DAMNATION

C.J. Henderson · Robert Hack

KOLCHAK:
The Night Stalker
the LOVECRAFTIAN
DAMNATION

story by
C.J. Henderson

illustrated by
Robert Hack

colored by
Evan Shaver

cover A by **Robert Hack**
cover B by **Doug Klauba**

edited by **Joe Gentile**   design by **Erik Enervold**

creative consultant: **Mark Dawidziak**

Kolchak created by **Jeff Rice**

Joe Gentile – editor-in-chief
Dave Ulanski – art director
Lori G – editorial
Rory Bautista, Tim Ganz,
Max Cockrell & Mike Reynolds
-ground control-
Richard Dean Star
-special projects coordinator-
Tim Lasiuta
-research & development-
Joe Gentile & Dave Ulanski
-publishers-

visit us on the web at www.moonstonebooks.com

"Oh man, I am so glad you could make it," said the man sitting behind the desk. "Really *so* glad. Because, trust me, if it's anyone I need in my hemisphere right now, it's the amazing Carl Kolchak."

The speaker was Marvin Richards, host of the curiously popular cable television news show, *Challenge of the Unknown*. Holding out his hand to the older man making his way forward into his office, he added, "My good and dear friend, you have no idea what's been going on around here."

Richards' guest was also a newsman, but even though they both often found themselves following stories involving the strange, the bizarre, and even the supernatural, they were not of a similar breed.

"Marv," answered Kolchak, taking the younger man's hand, shaking it, "you okay? You look a little green around the gills."

There were several differences between the two. The first was that while the older of the two stumbled across such events while looking for any kind of event to report, the younger was in the business of making the strange, the bizarre, and especially the supernatural, the news of the moment.

"Carl, I passed merely green at a run two days ago. Can I offer you a Scotch?"

"Thought you'd never ask."

Richards' show was a wildly popular one, but he did not seem at that moment much like the anchorman and producer of a wildly popular program. Indeed, during all of Kolchak's previous meetings with the television personality, the man had been the living embodiment of preening success. That was not the Marvin Richards sitting across from the reporter summoning his secretary at that moment. It was not the Richards who loved his chair solely because it was more expensive than the one the head of the network had in his office. This was a different Richards. A frightened one.

And a frightened Marvin Richards was something that worried Carl Kolchak more than a little.

"Bet you're wondering what I could want with you, why I'd drag your ass all the way up here to Burbank, eh Carl?"

The reporter eyed his host with a slight trace of suspicion, one so strong he could not hide it completely. For one thing, Burbank was not all that far from Kolchak's home turf of Hollywood. For another, men like Richards did not care how they inconvenienced others. Not unless they wanted something from them.

"Did cross my mind, Marv."

And then, the producer of *Challenge of the Unknown* did something which cued his guest that not only were things not right, but that they were as wrong as they could possibly be. When his secretary arrived with the drink Kolchak had been promised, the reporter took instant note of the bottle on the tray. Of course it was Scotch. Richards knew Kolchak's favorite lubricant, and like any good producer was certain to always oil a wheel he wanted running smoothly with the proper grease. But, it was not the Scotch that caught the reporter's eye, but the brand. Watching the golden liquid splash gently into his glass, Kolchak said nothing. He wanted to taste it first.

Accepting the offered snifter, he took a short sip, rolling the fluid around his mouth. He was greeted by a deep, smokey complex taste, a rich chocolate honey flavor that rounded out with a peaty finish that shivered his soul. Swallowing, he allowed himself another sip, a longer one, then set his snifter down on the desk before him.

"Okay, spill it, Marv. What in hell's going on around here, and what made you bring my tired old ass into it?"

"What do you mean, Carl?" Richards made his answer with a smooth, non-committal tone that would have misled most, but his guest knew him too well.

"Marvin, you're smooth." Picking up his snifter once more, Kolchak eyed it like a jewelry appraiser, saying, "but you're dealing with your elders here. First, clever of you to have your secretary keep the bottle's label turned from me, but she's too used to serving the good stuff in the right glasses. Last time I was here the Scotch was served in tumblers." Pointing toward the bottle on the desk, the reporter added;

"This ultra-fine tonsil cleaner is tasting a lot like Glen Fiddich to me. Maybe even the forty year old collection... twenty-five hundred a bottle last time I stared longingly at the Forbes tracking report on

Scotch prices." As Richards' eyes saddened, Kolchak took another loving sip, then gently demanded;

"You're a wonderful host, but let's get down to business. What's the deal, Marv? Last time I checked, nobody was pouring ninety-five dollar drinks for me unless they wanted something nobody else could deliver. And frankly, 'my good and dear friend,' I'm not sure I want to know what that could possibly be."

Kolchak watched as his host's face drew inward on itself. Lines sprouted across Richards' forehead no amount of makeup would be able to hide from the cameras. Tension forced itself down his arms, making his hands shake, fingers drum. Lifting his head to the reporter once more, the producer stared into Kolchak's eyes, telling him;

"We're going to die, Carl. We're all going to Hell and I don't think there's any escaping it."

"That's a very broad statement. Think you could give me a bit of the *why* you feel that way? Assuming you want good and dear me to help in some way."

"Don't joke," snapped Richards. "You're probably the only person who can help us—we *need* you, Carl."

Kolchak swallowed hard. The reporter was, in his soul, not a particularly brave individual. He had never gone to any great lengths to hide the fact. But, it had not been all that long ago when the producer had helped him out at a time when if he had not, the actual fate of the world might have come into question. Taking a deep pull from his snifter, Kolchak licked his lips, then said;

"All right. Calm down, go back to the beginning, and just tell me everything."

Richards gave his guest an odd glance, as if he had somehow forgotten who the reporter was—why he was there. Then, he ground his teeth for a moment, and started to speak.

"Do you remember Dr. Randel Penes?"

Kolchak froze. It was a suspension of movement which lasted but a moment, but it was a thing complete. His breathing, heart beat, eye movement–everything about him, all that made him a functioning human being–came to a sudden, complete halt. The reporter remembered Dr. Penes all too well. Despite his continual, futile attempts to forget.

It was Dr. Penes that had tricked the *Challenge of the Unknown* team into purchasing a copy of an ancient and terrible book. It was Dr. Penes who had used the unspeakable tome to summon a thing from

beyond which had murdered a score of people in a handful of seconds there in the very building where he and Richards were sipping Scotch.

Kolchak remembered everything about that hideous afternoon–the insidious odor that had filled the room, a nauseating mix of rotting honey and boiling tar–musky and reptilian. He remembered the sounds of people all about him heaving up their lunches, could once again taste the bile that invaded his own throat. He remembered the fear lurching through his nerves, and the vibrating sound of the air all around him as it began to shake itself apart. And, most of all, he remembered the growing gelatinous mass of iridescent blackness that had been spawned within their midst, which had swallowed souls like so many peanuts.

"What are you telling me," asked Kolchak. His voice an instant away from shattering, his knees aching with the sensation to force their owner to his feet, to pivot and head him toward the door, his entire body struggling to simply rise and flee, he forced himself to somehow remain calm enough to say;

"We got rid of him. Him and his thing, and the damn book he used to bring it here. They're gone. All three of them. Displaced, dismissed, sent back–*gone!*"

"I'm not so certain, Carl."

And then, Richards closed his eyes. His elbows on his desk, he shuddered as he dropped his head into his hands. Unable to control himself, the producer allowed himself to break down, to finally show the face so desperate to break free. Lifting his head, tears streaming his cheeks, he stared unblinking at the reporter across the desk from him and blurted;

"I don't think we got rid of him after all."

"You mean ..."

"I mean, he's coming back."

The building dread Kolchak had been feeling slammed against his heart. Blood pumping furiously, he rose from his chair, sat down again, stood up again, then froze in a crouching position. Fear thundering through his nervous system, he grabbed at the back of the chair in which he had been sitting, then blurted;

"What are you talking about? He can't come back–that's *impossible!*" The reporter swung his head back and forth, the back of his mind trying to find something for him to look at which would not remind him of where he was or anything he had just heard. Desperation clawing it's way into his mind, he then

asked weakly;

"Isn't it?"

Standing, Richards grabbed up his drink and threw back its remaining contents. The producer considered how much he had swallowed, then picked up the bottle of Glen Fiddich and refilled his snifter. Doing the same for his quest without asking, Richards then took another healthy gulp. Kolchak followed his example. Then, after both of them had calmed their nerves at least slightly, the producer said;

"Crazy stuff has been happening around here. I could just tell you what's been happening, but ...

I might as well show you. We've got some of it on tape." The two men stared at each other for a moment–neither moving, neither speaking. Finally, Richards added;

"Carl, listen to me. I'm scared. I flat out admit it–okay? I just want to show you what we know, see what you think. I mean, you remember Penes. If this is what we think it is, if he and his puddle of doom are making their way back here, you know who he's going to want to pay back first, don't you?"

Kolchak nodded. It had been he who had thwarted the doctor's plans. Penes had tricked the

studio into securing an ancient text for him, a volume he called the *Kitah al-Azif*, among other names. It was a thing known throughout history as the *Cultus Maleficarum, Liber Logaeth, Necronomicon Ex Mortis* and several dozen other names. It was most commonly referred to as the Necronomicon, however, the ultimate book of dark wisdom. Penes had felt humanity too sick to be allowed to continue to exist, and had planned to unleash countless dark terrors into the world to bring about the end of mankind.

The simple, tiny speck of horror he had unleashed in the Burbank studio had slaughtered eighteen people in but a handful of moments. More would have doubtlessly followed.

For indeed, so bizarre, so beyond the mind of mortal consciousness was the thing Penes unleashed, that men and women had simply stood and stared into its boiling darkness, stupefied-transfixed. Utterly past they ability to comprehend, their minds unable to interpret the evidence fed them by their eyes, they allowed themselves to be swallowed and consumed, their bodies evaporated, souls devoured.

All except Kolchak.

The reporter was not an overly brave man, but he was a practical one. He was also a man unique in the world. Unlike most normal, rational, sensible people, Carl Kolchak believed in things others did not. Vampires and werewolves. Witches and Satan. Bog monsters, ghosts, banshees and aliens from

other worlds. He had good reason to believe in such things, of course. He believed because he had seen them all. And, moreover, had survived them all.

Armed with the knowledge that there really were things that went bump in the night, the reporter had managed to separate Penes from his demonic text, and then tossed it and then the doctor himself into the monstrous presence making its way into the studio.

Which was why as he stared into Richards' eyes, he found himself unable to answer the producer's question. Yes, he understood that Penes would wish him the most terrible, blistering of revenges. But, he had watched the man be absorbed by a horror from beyond. The doctor had been dissolved along with his hideous book and his creature banished. Summoning, if not his courage, at least his curiosity, Kolchak finally said;

"Marv, I don't get it. Penes was atomized. So was his damn Necronomicon for that matter—we saw it."

"I know."

"Well then, before I scare my own hair into turning white, please tell me, what makes you think this boob has any chance of touching us again?"

"Good points, Carl. I mean it. I said the same things. But sadly, I've got some good answers.

You ready to come see those tapes I was talking about?"

The reporter hesitated for a moment, his natural caution crawling out of hiding, whispering to him to run for the door while he had the chance. Then, common sense reminding him that if the monstrous Dr. Penes actually did manage to return to the world of the living that he, Carl Kolchak, would most assuredly be his first victim, he sighed heavily, then asked;

"Can we take the bottle with us?"

"Carl," answered Richards, grabbing up the Scotch-in-question as he came around his desk, "Believe me, I have no plans whatsoever of spending a single minute sober until this crap is over."

"Then," Kolchak said, shaking his head sadly, "lay on, MacDuff. Show me what you got."

The producer led his guest to a video editing room on a lower floor. A technician the reporter thought he remembered was sitting, nervously drumming his fingers, obviously waiting for them to arrive. When the man took note of their entrance, he said;

"All ready, Mr. Richards." Then, his manner noticeably improving, he added, "good to see you again,

Mr. Kolchak."

The reporter's first instinct was to question the younger man, to play humble about what he might be able to bring to the situation. Truthfully, Kolchak had been wondering throughout his conversation with Richards as to what he might be able to accomplish. He was grateful that the producer had decided to include him. If Richards was correct and Penes had not died, then he would assuredly be correct about what the doctor's plans might be as well.

Looking into the editor's eyes, Kolchak was about to dismiss the younger man's hopes when he suddenly stopped himself. The fellow had literally been shaking in his seat when the reporter had entered the room. Just seeing Kolchak, however, had noticeably calmed him. Not enjoying the implied responsibility, but realizing they needed people who could focus, who would not freeze in panic, the reporter swallowed his own fear, answering;

"Good to see you, too. Marv here tells me you guys have been having some kind of problem with an old friend of ours or something?"

The younger man shuddered slightly, then found a dollop of courage in Kolchak's nonchalant attitude. Nodding his head, the editor actually managed a weak grin, then said;

"Or something. Yeah. Should I show him what we've got, Mr. Richards?"

The producer nodded, taking another healthy slug from his snifter. Offering the bottle to Kolchak, the reporter filled his own, knocked back a gulp, then began pouring again while the editor worked at the control board in front of him. After only a few seconds of moving dials and toggles, he said;

"Okay, I'm starting us out with a bit of video we should all remember. Just to reestablish the scene."

Kolchak gulped as the over-sized monitor before them flashed with color, showing him images he had hoped never to see again.

There on the screen was Dr. Randel Penes. The reporter felt no shame in having winced at the sight. Everyone in the room had done so, unable to control themselves as the sight of the slight, small man flashed before them.

The older images played out in less than ninety seconds. Richards had wanted something for the group of them to focus upon, to jog their memories. The studio security cameras had been rolling, of course, when Penes had summoned his monster. Two of the show's cameramen had been rolling at the time as well. Between the four views they had all the footage they could have ever wanted of that

terrible moment.

Penes first laying eyes on the Necronomicon the show had procured. Penes opening the dimensional portal which allowed his thing, the Nyogtha, access to the studio. Then, the arrival of the shapeless evil, the living darkness that slaughtered eighteen people before it was returned to its own side of the wall between worlds. Eleven of those brutal moments had been captured on film. Reading his display, the editor cued a new piece of footage, saying;

"All right, that's what we all saw. Now, here's some of what we've been seeing lately."

The new image sent to the monitor was darker than that which had just been viewed. The studio it showed appeared to be closed for the evening, only the most basic of security lights burning.

"This is from, what, when was it," asked Richards, "last Monday? Tuesday?"

"Tuesday," answered the editor, pointing at the time and date coding in a lower corner of the screen. Speaking to Kolchak, he added, "watch the background on the left-hand side. See that glow? Okay, watch that."

The reporter stared, noting the beginnings of a spectral shimmer. It was not anything

tremendous. No more light than that given off by a very low-powered flashlight. It held no particular shape, did not suggest any kind of eventual form. But, it was *something*, and it was a something that did not seemed easily explained.

"I'm assuming you checked the possibility of natural light sources--yes?"

"Yes, Carl," answered Richards. Taking a healthy slug from his snifter, the producer added, "security made a routine check when they saw this the next morning. Even if something within the studio had somehow been turned on without anyone there, it still wouldn't give off a result like that."

"What would?"

"Show him."

The editor killed the one feed, replacing it with another. Kolchak checked the time code, noting that they were watching footage taken by the same camera some twenty-four hours later. As he knew it would, the scene shown was the same as the one previous, with some slight differences. This time, the shimmer was brighter. This time, it lasted longer. And this time, it did not appear quite as insubstantial as it had previously.

"Just wait," said the editor with a nervous laugh, as if reading the reporter's mind, "it gets better."

The next shot from the same camera, captured roughly twenty-four hours after the second, one

that furthered the forward progression. At much the same time it showed the same pulsating light, once again shining brighter, once again lasting longer. Once again seeming somewhat less formless.

"Here's that better I promised."

The next shot introduced to the screen had been taken in by a different camera, one shooting in color. Men and women in white coats were bustling around the area where the shimmer had appeared previously. All of them held what appeared to be electronic measuring devices. All of them appeared extremely serious. Then suddenly, a somber Marvin Richards stepped into view.

"We're here in Studio 12 in our own Burbank production facilities where we're investigating an as-yet unclassified phenomenon. For the past few days–"

The Richards standing in the editing room made a hand gesture which the editor understood as an order to kill the sound. Watching his still unsuspecting self on the screen, the producer said, "we were very happy then. Thought how lucky we were. For once we didn't have to go out looking for strange. The damn shit was coming to us. Like an audition."

Richards giggled at his moment of humor. Then, the scene on the monitor skipped ahead in time, and there was nothing further to prompt comedy. As previously, the shimmer began again, neatly

contained within the area of the studio carefully marked off with crowd control poles and belting. But, something new had been added. This time, the room was not empty. This time it was flooded with light, every corner holding people. Warm flesh, pulsing with life, filled with blood.

It was all that was needed.

The glow did exactly what Richards had hoped. It stretched its size in all directions once more. But then, suddenly it solidified for the briefest of instances.

For a split second, the glare darkened to black, a shimmering obsidian mass which lashed out, tendrils of it flashing past the ridiculous barriers set around it. Before anyone even realized what was happening, the ebony lengths snared two of the actors pretending to be scientists and dragged them across the room into the main body of the manifestation.

All was over before any of the others could react. Indeed, if the event had not been captured on multiple cameras, none present would even have been able to accurately describe what had transpired. Every millimeter of footage was studied, however, and that was when the most terrifying discovery of

all was made. While the editor punched up the code needed to show the next piece of tape, Richards said;

"Yeah, those people are gone. No one heard about it because no one's been told. Luckily for us they were both unmarried. No one in their lives to ask any immediate questions. We're letting sleeping dogs lie for now."

"'Luckily.'" Kolchak repeated the word, unable to say it without a tone of shock and recrimination. "'Luckily?'"

"Don't judge me, Carl," snapped the producer, his own tone straining. "Let me see if I get to live myself before I goddamn complicate my life with police reports. Oh ... and the media."

"This is the shot you'll want to see, Mr. Kolchak."

The reporter turned from Richards, looking at the monitor once more. The editor explained that during their studying of the apparition, one of the techniques they had used was slowing the footage down. At one point, they had discovered the still shot with which he had filled the monitor. Kolchak stared at the image for only a moment before he had to sit back in his chair, suddenly too weak to hold himself steady in an upright position. Draining his snifter without realizing he had done so, the reporter pointed at the screen before him, shouting;

"Penes! Jesus Christ—that was Penes!"

Following his own finger, Kolchak stared at the image, dreading it, unable to turn away. Almost unable to believe his eyes, he studied the horror before him. He was seeing Dr. Randel Penes, of that he had no doubt. But it was a Penes not human. It was a Penes who had merged with his terrible creature. And what was worse, the reporter realized, they had the book.

"They've got the book?" Kolchak practically howled his words. "How in God's name could they have the book?"

"We saw it dissolve, right there on that floor. We saw it fall apart, atom by atom. What are they doing with, how could, when did ..." And then, what little steam he had remaining draining from his system, the reporter slouched in his chair, holding out his glass, demanding;

"I need a drink."

As Richards poured, his cell phone began vibrating. Handing the bottle to Kolchak, the producer pulled his phone from his belt, drunkenly talking into the wrong end of it until his editor took it away from him and then handed it back right-side-up. He listened for a moment, then told whoever was at the

other end that they "would be right there." When asked where they were going, he answered, Studio 12. The ladies are here."

Utterly confused, Kolchak asked, "What ladies?"

"That Dr. Helms of yours, and someone she brought along."

"Helms is here," muttered the reporter. "Oh, Jesus, Mary and Joseph, now I need a big drink."

Kolchak drained his snifter, fully intending to pour himself another. Halfway to doing so, however, he thought for a moment of how exactly Helms would receive him if he arrived three-sheets-to-the-wind. The professor would not care, of course, that he had been drinking. The petty vices in which most people indulged did not disturb her. But, he told himself, she would most certainly have more than one stinging comment to make over the fact that he would dull his reflexes in a situation like the one they were in at that moment.

And then, the truth of that particular moment struck him. Or, more precisely, the fact that he probably did not actually know what was going on in the least. Suddenly he realized, he had come up to Burbank thinking there might be a job opportunity ahead of him. Now, as he thought on the swirl of events he was being shown, he had no idea of what was happening. Placing both his snifter and

the bottle of Glen Fiddich on the console before him, Kolchak tapped his host on the shoulder, asking;

"Marv, just what the hell is going on here?

"What'dya mean, Carl?"

"I mean, what's going on? Why am I here? What do you want of me, in this place? At this time? Why is Helms here? In other words, you devious son'va bitch, what are you up to this time?"

"Oh, sorry. Thought it was obvious. We're gonna set a trap for Penes. Give him the old one-two before he breaks through and, like, I don't know... destroys the world or somethin'."

Richards stared blankly at Kolchak as if the reporter were a half-witted child who could not be trusted with round-tipped scissors. A score of reactions rang within Kolchak's brain, all of them screaming to be answered. He wanted to grab up the Scotch once more and drain the bottle. He wanted to head for the front door, wanted to strangle the producer, to scream and wail in frustration, to pray. He especially wanted to pray.

He could not, however, for the fact that after all he had seen and survived over the past few years, he simply had no idea who or what one could pray to any more.

Lowering his head, Kolchak closed his eyes, taking several deep, cleansing breaths. Then, feeling as prepared as possible for the horror ahead of him, knowing that in the end he realistically had no other choice, he said;

"All right, let's go. Let's not keep the ladies waiting."

It only took the trio of men some eleven minutes to reach Studio 12. Once inside, Kolchak greeted his old instructor and occasional friend, Dr. Kirsten Helms. She was a thin, plain woman of medium height, one who had looked ancient when he had first met her in his college days. The years had not improved her overall appearance any. But, as old as the doctor appeared, it was as nothing compared to the black woman waiting with her.

"Mr. Richards, Carl," Helms said quietly, flashing Kolchak a disapproving glare as she did so, "I'd like you to meet someone I believe can help us, Madame Sarna La Rainelle."

"Wh-What?" The producer stuttered the single word as if to imply he doubted his hearing. Instantly sobering to an amazing degree, his eyes went wide as he rattled on in honest amazement;

"Sarna La *Rainelle*? Paddy Moran, from Bullfinches, he told me all about you. You, you've known all the greats–right. Like you worked with John Legrasse–more than once. And Anton Zarnak... you

were there when he escaped the Tindolosi. Oh my god, you knew Marc Thorner, didn't you? And Ravenwood, Jules de Grandin, and, and that ninja mystic... what was his name–"

"Koji Matsuriki was a noble man who served humanity well."

The woman's voice was a thin and raspy thing, the tattered remains of a once fine silk. She was well dressed in a classic sense–long skirt, high collar, proper gloves. Her net-veiled hat covered her fiercely silver hair, as well as her deeply-lined face, but despite her camouflage, still her age screamed outward in her every movement. She was an ancient presence, and although he could not say why exactly, Kolchak found himself comforted by her presence.

Turning away from the others, the older woman moved across the room to the spot where Penes would appear in a few hours. As she did, Helms said, "I'm glad you're here, Carl. You'll give this Penes something to focus on. Give us a chance to snare him while his beast is gnawing on you."

"What? Like a stake-out goat? That's all I am here?"

"You listen to me, Carl Kolchak," snapped the doctor, her tone ringing with the authority of the classroom, "I've been told what happened here. I've seen the footage. I know what happened isn't your fault. If anything, your bumbling efforts might have saved the world—"

"Now, don't go making me out some kind of hero ..."

"Stop it!" Kolchak froze, the genial smile that had been forming on his face slinking out of sight. "Penes wanted the Necronomicon to bring about the end of humanity. He said so, and you stopped him. He's focused on you now. He has to be. When he comes through tonight, if you're here, he won't notice anything else. Not right away."

"No, of course not," responded the reporter. "Maybe there will be all of three, four seconds before he realizes what's going on. Of course, I'll be dead by then, but the rest of you will have your three or four seconds—"

"You coward." Helms snapped the words off bitterly. "How can you only think of yourself at a time like this? You know the power we're dealing with here. After that business in Rogers, even a slack-jawed reprobate such as yourself should understand what's about to be unleashed. You're not just some simple mundane fool wandering the streets–you *know!*"

"Yes, you're right, professor," Kolchak answered, his voice tired and small. "I do know. I thought I'd seen something in my time, waltzing around with vampires and mummies, werewolves, all the other Universal monsters Abbott and Costello met ... but this Nyogtha thing, and like you said,

everything I learned after that... this makes things like zombies and witches seem like, like ..."

"Like nothing."

All in the room turned at the sound of Madame La Rainelle's voice. Turning from her work, she pulled her tired body up from the floor, wiping her gloved hands one against the other as she said;

"You done learned the secret, haven't you, Mr. Kolchak? You know now there be no god for this world, not a one who cares if we live or die, anyway. There be no white-bearded man sitting on a cloud, keeping a Santa Claus list of our sins."

Moving forward toward the reporter, the woman moved as fast as her advanced years would allow, her still-keen eyes focused on him as she said;

"You've learned the world is not the center of creation, that we be living on a small, insignificant speck on the edge of an indifferent universe, that our lives are not meant to be anything more than brutish, inconsequential, and all too short. And, like most people, you're understandably having a speck of trouble dealing with that notion. Yes?"

Kolchak, suddenly feeling almost completely sober, swallowed hard, then answered the old woman.

"Lady, I've known all that for a long time. A lot of people have. Then again, I willing to bet that every once in a while, even you have some trouble dealing with that idea. Don't you?"

La Rainelle tilted her head back so as to be able to stare directly into Kolchak's eyes. She did so for only a moment, then turned toward Dr. Helms. Her mouth spreading into a wide and seductive grin, she said;

"I like this one." Turning back to the reporter, she poked him gently in the side with a single finger, telling him, "You remind me of ol' Legrasse. He was a tough one, too, had him some real meat on his soul. You a better man than you know, Carl Kolchak."

"Yeah," responded the reporter, smiling slightly himself. "Send my boss Tony a memo to that effect, would you?"

"Let's see about living through the night, then I let you know."

"Well, if that's the case," said Kolchak, turning back to Dr. Helms, "then maybe someone should try bringing me up to speed. I mean, okay, you're right. Terrifying as the concept is of being here when that maniac arrives, I'd want to get my hands on me if I were him, so yeah, best to meet him head on. But, c'mon, just what the hell is it we're going to be meeting?"

"You refer to the creature in the videos," answered Helms. "I won't waste time hedging since there isn't anyone here who doesn't accept the fantastic. The Nyogtha and Penes were thrown

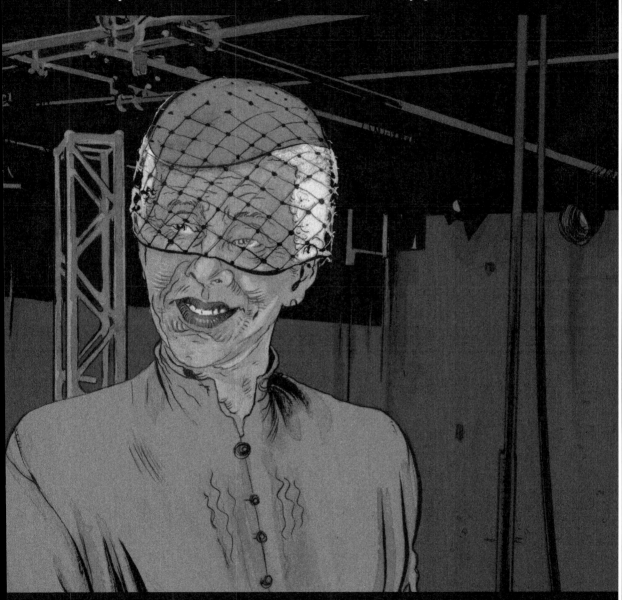

together in the center of a dimensional rift. It seems obvious their bodies have merged. Which means we're talking about an nearly all-powerful creature that now possesses intelligence."

"And," added Madame La Rainelle, "it got the book, too."

"But how is that even possible?" Kolchak folded his arms across his chest, his entire manner that of one who had simply been asked to accept too much. Knowing what he had seen in the video clips, but unable to accept it, he demanded, pointing at the floor, "*how* could he have the damn book?

"We saw it dissolve. Right there, where that stain is. How can he have something that no longer exists?"

"This be a hard concept for any to accept," answered La Rainelle, "but you must. De Necronomicon, it not like any other book there ever been. And this one you saw, this wasn't one of the countless translations that float around the world. The ones in Latin, German, Japanese even, they can be dealt with, they be just paper and ink and glue. But the one our Mr. Richards here had the Middle East combed for, the one Penes directed him toward, that was the real thing–that was the one penned and

bound in human flesh by Abdul Alhazred."

"And, Carl," interrupted Helms, "understand, as intensely as this book and its author have been studied, we know practically nothing about them for certain. For one thing, the name Alhazred means nothing in Arabic. His real name might have been Abd al-Azrad, or Abdallah Zahr-ad-Din, or possibly Abd Al-'Uzza. Many think that ..."

"Ahhhhh, Professor," countered Kolchak, his expression caught half-way between amusement and frustration, "maybe we could leave the more esoteric classroom stuff for later, just concentrate on the book for now. You know, get our lives saved first–little stuff like that."

Dr. Helms sighed, not so much over the reporter's lack of interest in the wealth of details she could provide, but in having been caught indulging her academic nature at the expense of their own survival. Nodding, she answered;

"Good point. Even the worst of students can sometimes have an intelligent comment. Broken clocks being correct at least twice a day. Very well. The book."

"Our problem here," the doctor explained, "is that we're dealing with the actual, hand-written, first-ever edition of the most powerful magical tome ever penned. When Alhazred tried to destroy it, he himself was torn apart in broad daylight in the streets of Damascus."

"By the book?"

"No, Mr. Richards," came Helms' flat, somewhat annoyed answer. "By its servitors. Think of any magical device. The Ouija board, for instance. Pick one up in a novelty store, use it all you like, it's doubtful you'll even reach your maiden aunt Tilly. But, get your hands on one of the originals, the dark wood boards carved in the forests of Gaul, blessed by the prophets of Verindor... let's just say your results should be different."

"So, this copy of the Necronomicon, it *can't* be destroyed?"

"No, Carl," answered the doctor. "There are too many dark forces bound to this particular volume. It's destruction would take the intervention of a god, or someone willing to throw that much power around."

"That's why it's been sequestered so often. The Knights Templar were formed by Comte de Champagne to guard it. Before that, Constantine had it hidden away in the Imperial Library of Constantinople."

"These be true words she speaks." All heads turned toward Madame La Rainelle. She had returned to the preparations she had been making inside the roped off area of the studio floor. Looking as if she had finished her work, she rose from the floor once more, saying;

"This book need be kept from the world, outside its reach, as often as possible. You see, the evil

that got its grip so firm upon it, it needs a soul to defy it, to bind it. To own it. The book, it don't care who be holding onto it, long as *somebody* be holding onto it."

"The problem is, however," added Dr. Helms, making her way over toward La Rainelle to view her progress, "the *somebody* that owns it right now, is Randel Penes. And if he makes it back to this plane of existence, bound molecularly to Nyogtha, and in possession of the Necronomicon–"

"Then we can all just bend over and kiss our asses goodbye–right?" Smiling, Madame La Rainelle reached out, touching the doctor's shoulder gently as she said;

"I told you I like this boy."

"Try teaching him something," snapped Helms. "That might change your opinion."

"Hey," snapped Kolchak, molding his face into a frown, "I'm right here, you know."

"Well, loud boy," answered the elder witch woman, pointing toward an area outside the barriers within which she had been working, "now you want to be over here. It be time to start."

"Start what, may I ask?" Crossing the room, the reporter stared at the markings La Rainelle had made on the floor, He also took note of the various carved pieces of stone she had placed at various strategic points. "Or don't I want to know?"

"Right to the point," interrupted Richards. Filling his snifter once more with the last of the Scotch, he added, "a Carl Kolchak trademark. And a good one. Professor, you told me on the phone this was going to be dangerous. And that we'd need some muscle. Is it time?"

"Yes," replied the doctor, her tone firm, but laced with trepidation. "You'd better get your cannon fodder in here."

As Kolchak watched, wishing he had hung onto the bottle of Glen Fiddich, Richards made a call on his cell phone, instructing someone on the other end to "send in the boys."

Before the reporter could ask about who "the boys" might be, a precise clamor was heard coming from the main hallway. Seconds later, ten heavily-armed men and three women entered the room on a trot, followed by a last man pushing a large flatbed stacked high with containers hidden by a large, heavy canvas. Instructed to "fall in" next to the wall, ten of the men and all the women did so without question as their obvious leader turned to Richards.

"Ready for work, sir." Turning to the others, the producer waved a hand toward the newcomers, explaining;

"Mercs By The Hour. Meet Captain Ted Reed, creator of the best pro-active security/defense organization in the business."

"So Captain, you think these fellows of yours," asked Kolchak, hurried adding, "and ladies, will be able to handle what's coming? What we're looking to trap isn't exactly your garden variety terrorist, you know."

"We've been made well aware of what we're going to be up against, Mr. Kolchak." As the reporter raised one eyebrow, the squad leader added, "we were briefed on who all would be here, as well as the opposition."

"And you're prepared to face what for lack of a better description, is a *god?*"

"Let's just say we've come up with a few, ah ... shall we say ... radical ideas on keeping this thing contained."

"Radical ideas?" Kolchak squinted, staring at the man intently, trying to discern what the phrase he had just quoted might actually mean. Not able to pull the answer for which he was searching from out of the air, he began to inquire further, but his voice was lost as both Richards and the squad leader began barking orders. The producer was getting his camera people in place while the Reed was

busy positioning his people.

Standing to the side, Kolchak found his mind spinning. Shutting his eyes, the reporter concentrated for a moment on what was about to happen. He was joined with people preparing to defy a god. Helms had told him Nyogtha was a minor deity. In his time he had faced werewolves and vampires, zombies and witches, ghosts and mummies, but a god? A *god?* This was new. This was different. This... this was insane.

Kolchak opened his eyes, wondering how and why he had ended up in the situation he was in at that moment. Years earlier he had been fearless enough to call out a major political machine. For his troubles he had been blacklisted from every major print outlet in the country.

After making a comfortable enough living for himself in Las Vegas, he had stumbled across another story everyone else had wanted to ignore. He had faced that situation as well. He had dug into his soul and found the courage to stand against the authorities once more to stop a vampire. He had shown courage on multiple levels. Not only had he faced a fear, the mere thought of which paralyzed most into a frozen immobility, but he had also faced official censor, ridicule, and the threat of imprisonment. In the end he had stopped an evil hundreds of years old and saved who knew how many innocent lives in the process. For his trouble he had been run out of town, the first of a series of towns.

"And now," he thought, "I'm down to my last chance. I've got nowhere else to go if I lose the lousy job I've got now. I've got no home, no kids, no real friends... nobody at all. What I do have is a lunatic son of a bitch who wants me dead, who's got the power of a monster god and the most dangerous black magic in the universe to help him make it happen." Narrowing his eyes to slits, the reporter frowned, then muttered;

"Why me, God? Tell me... why is it always me?"

"They say he works in mysterious ways," answered Dr. Helms. As Kolchak turned toward her, she continued, adding, "if he can allow the last half-dozen presidential elections turn out the way he did, where's the surprise in him expecting heroism out of you?"

The reporter gave Helms a sinister grimace, then began to speak, only to be cut-off by Richards' voice booming through the studio loudspeakers. Apparently La Rainelle had put her summoning into effect and everyone needed to take their places. As several of the mercenaries began uncovering their flatbed, the rest took up defensive positions around the witch woman. Helms slapped Kolchak

on the back of the head, reminding him he was supposed to stay out of sight until called out.

As La Rainelle read from her book, a noxious, terrifying odor began to permeate the room. The same glimmer that had appeared on the night security tapes shown in the center of the roped off area flashed dully, a wavering filled with sordid, nauseating colors. And then, after only a handful of seconds, a horrid wave of iridescent blackness broke through the undulating static, a thing neither liquid nor solid, except in its center, where the undulating, gelatinous mass was merged with the skeletal body of Professor Randel Penes.

"Now!"

At Reed's order, several of his squad began sliding cages across the floor, aimed directly at Nyogtha/Penes. Inside each one were cats, dogs and other animals. As Kolchak watched in horror, the blob of living darkness before him began throwing out tentacle-like pseudopods, snaring the cages and drawing them into its mass. The animals appeared drugged, for they made no noises of protest as they were absorbed, cages and all.

While this continued, the reporter stared at Penes. Strands of Nyogtha appeared to be piercing his flesh at every possible point. His fingers, genitals, toes, neck, all seemed completely merged with the

god-thing. The horror, Kolchak could tell, had been caught off guard. It had not expected to break completely back into the world this time. And now, with its inhuman side distracted by the fresh lives being offered to it, the pair were not reacting as quickly as they might.

"But," thought the reporter, "where's the damn book?"

"Kolchak." The single word hissed out of Penes' mouth, the tone of it resembling the sound of rats dying in the rain, "I hear you thinking, Carl Kolchak."

The Nyogtha/Penes thing turned in the reporter's direction, but by then, the damage had been done. Seeing the last of their containers sliding into the swirling black mass in the center of the room,

Reed depressed a red toggle on the control box in his hand. In reaction, the obsidian mass shuddered, flame and noise belching through its body in a score of spots.

As an acrid black smoke filled the studio, Richards shouted, "That's right, Penes. Your partner swallowed our offerings like they were going out of style, but only the first few were alive! After that it was suckin' down sculpted meat filled with bombs and poison. Back to Hell for you, Randy!"

"Perhaps."

All froze at the sound of the single word.

"Nyogtha does seem to have suffered some damage. But it's nothing a good meal won't cure."

And then, a half-dozen pseudopods lashed outward from the darkness, snagging four of the mercenaries. Before anyone could react, the quartet were pulled backward into the still pulsating shimmer in the middle of the smoke. Two of them had the time to scream before they were gone.

"Best target," shouted Reed. "Fire!"

Their leader's voice refocusing their attention, the remaining mercenaries aimed for the center of the black void before them and opened fire, sending bullets and grenades into the smoke and fire.

Reed raced forward, pulling Madame La Rainelle behind a protective barrier. He was not afraid of any of his people shooting her by mistake, but he had no way of telling where any of the shrapnel from the grenades might end up. For a moment, however, it seemed as if such considerations did not matter. As the smoke from the initial attack finally began to dissipate, the Nyogtha/Penes thing came sliding forward.

"You really have no idea what you face now, do you?"

"Why don't you tell us?"

"Carl Kolchak," Penes said. "Out in the open. Ready to face your end for daring to defy me?"

"I never defied you," answered the reporter. Walking forward with his hands in his pockets, he said, "I mean-

-you? You're nothing. Even that lump of licorice you've decided to make your significant other, is no real threat."

His eyes spinning like pinwheels, mad flecks of energy bleeding from his tear ducts, what remained of the professor laughed, then shouted;

"You're utterly mad."

"Not really," answered Kolchak matter-of-factly. "Just smart enough to know my real enemy. Screw you, Penes. I mean, who are you? Just some dink. I mean, you're nothing without the Necronomicon and you know it."

And then, the horror in the center of Studio 12 began to convulse. Reaching within itself, Nyogtha/Penes searched for a moment, and then pulled forth the horrid tome from deep within its bowels. Holding the hideous scripture above its head, the thing was about to speak further when Captain Reed gave two of his people who had been holding back the signal for which they had been waiting.

Firing their grapples, both struck the volume, one managing to actually ensnare it. Jerking his weapon, the mercenary pulled the Necronomicon free from the monstrosity's grasp. As he did so, the thing snarled madly, then threw forth two score of its pseudopods in a desperate attempt to regain the stolen book. It was too late.

Even as Kolchak dove for cover, all of the remaining mercenaries opened fire. Lead ricocheted about the room, much of it merely passing through the terrible obsidian shape. Changing tactics, the mercenaries switched to rifle grenades and incendiary charges. The Nyogtha bellowed, the creature forming its own mouth

independent of Penes'.Writhing in pain, the creature threw itself outward. Expanding its shape, the horror snared three more of the mercenaries and dragged to their deaths. Those remaining, however, continued their attack. At a signal from Reed, two of his soldiers that had been standing by with a set of vintage flame throwers stepped forward. Depressing their triggers, the men showered the monster with gallons of napalm, filling the studio with a harsh smell, a gagging stench halfway between that of rotting bodies and burning tar.

After several minutes of such aggravation, Nyogtha, no longer bound to obey its human burden, spit Randel Penes from its body. Free of the wretched burden it had dispised for so long, the terror emitted one last hideous screech, then allowed itself to be pulled back beyond the breech by Madame La Rainelle's spell of rejection.

What remained of Penes died before it hit the floor.

Several hours later, Studio 12 had calmed down considerably. A cleaning crew had removed all traces of the battle. Madame La Rainelle and Dr. Helms, as well as Reed and his remaining mercenaries had been treated for any injuries and then sent off with whatever compensation they had been promised.

Sitting in Marv Richards' office, the Necronomicon on the desk between them, the producer and Kolchak were most of the way through a second bottle of Glen Fiddich when the reporter said;

"You know, I'm going to have to take that damn book with me."

"I know."

"You remember what Helms, and your witch lady, both had to say about it. Someone has to own it. Someone who can resist it. Who won't use it."

"It'll bite your soul, Carl—you know that—every damned minute of every damn day you have left on Earth."

"Hey," shrugged the reporter, "I'm used to it."

Kolchak stared at the Scotch in his hand. In its swirling ripples he saw all that he had lost during his life, watched all he could not have spin round and round. Then, sighing, he drained his snifter and refilled it, then held it aloft, saying;

"To what might have been, Marv."

The two men tapped their glasses, then emptied them. Finally, after a bit more chatter, Kolchak slid the most dangerous book ever written into his bag and headed for the door, forcing himself to ignore the greedy whispers filtering past the layers of intoxication with which he had fortified himself, beguiling him, begging him to pull the book out of his bag. To open it, to read it, to plunge the world into madness. And to damn the soul he had fought so hard to protect.

As they would every damned minute of every damn day he had left on Earth. •